…Two more mortars go off at the same time behind me, but I only see a single hole. I pause and stare over my shoulder into the light. The other shot must have been directed toward a different tunnel. That can only mean one thing—they don't know where I am.

"We lost him, Commander." I clearly hear the deep, mechanical voice somewhere below me.

I place my ear against the tunnel floor.

"Launch the Tocsins, Soldier."

"Launching the Tocsins, Commander."

Before I even have time to react, four more explosions go off in all directions around me, one after the other.

Boom! Boom! Boom! Boom!

At first there is an ominous silence, but it only lasts for a second at the most. It's overpowered by an immediate silver light illuminating the entire tunnel where I lay helplessly. A piercing, high-pitched ringing follows that takes over the entire air duct. I close my one open eye and attempt to lift my head, but I can't even force myself to do that. A deafening, screeching sound has filled my entire body. I'm paralyzed. I try to lift my head off the tunnel floor again, but it feels like it weighs a thousand pounds.

I force open my eye, and the tunnel is spinning. I see double, triple everything. Move, I order myself. My head lolls to the side, and I can sense my lunch from earlier wanting to make another appearance. My head feels like it's about to implode. I squeeze out a tiny, low groan while still attempting to cup both of my hands over my ears in agony. I lose my balance; my head bangs up against the side of the tunnel wall.

I freeze.

I just gave myself away…

OTHER BOOKS BY R. L. MCDANIEL

The Big Hoot

LEVITATION

R. L. MCDANIEL

In loving memory of Uncle Lou
More than an uncle, a writing mentor

PROLOGUE

"Breaking news...another Tele attack in the Sol district today where a group of Teles robbed a bank; severely injuring seven innocent bystanders in the process."

A video begins on my Receiver's screen—the electronic device strapped around my wrist—of a car magically hovering ten feet off the ground, before rocketing over a busy street and smacking itself into the side of a gas truck innocently parked at a red light. A chorus of screams from a group of onlookers immediately follows the explosion, all conveniently filmed by numerous nearby security cameras in the area.

"A group of masked, unknown Teles," the news reporter continues, "created a diversion by luring all incoming drones to this location on the corner of 30th and 3rd. In the meantime, at least four other known Teles robbed First Governed Bank only two blocks over, getting away with almost three-point-nine million dollars in a matter of seconds."

"Oh, will you put that away?" my mom says, attempting to sound stern. "We're trying to eat without hearing about how screwed up the world is with all of those freaks running around moving things with their minds." She takes a long sip of the drink in front of her.

"This is already the ninth Tele-related attack this month in the Sol district."

"Nicholas, Listen to your mother." My father's attention comes back to the dinner table. He has two permanent dark rings underneath his eyes from working late practically every night this month; tonight being the first time he has been home for dinner in weeks.

"That's why we're here to remind you,—a jingle begins—if you see...something, say...something!"

Without looking up, I click the video off button on the side of my Receiver before shoveling in a large forkful of mashed potatoes and beans into my mouth. I press the side of my fork down into an end corner of a drab piece of dark meat on my plate, covered in grizzle and fat, attempting to tear off a bite.

A yellow light glows from across the table, pulling my eyes away from the center of my plate. My older brother Rollins's Receiver flashes on and off, signaling an incoming text.

I look across the table and get a glimpse of the message, just as Rollins turns the strapped device toward him to read:

———

Warehouse 8:00

———

An image from a couple of months ago, of Rollins walking into a downtown abandoned warehouse, flashes through my head. Above the door, half of the name Mitchell—for Mitchell's Warehouse—had faded away over time to where it now only read: hell's Warehouse. I can picture Rollins looking over his shoulder before entering the shabby, run-down building, checking to see if he had been followed. He was wearing sunglasses and a hat, but I know it was him.

Rollins wipes at the side of his mouth with the back of his hand before pushing back in his seat, scraping the chair's legs loudly across the tiled floor. He's wearing the same baseball cap he had on *that* day—his lucky, faded garnet hat with the letter S stitched across the center of it. "Gotta go. Study group."

Mom stares into the drink in front of her, knowing this has been happening more and more in recent days. Dad nods his head in approval, knowing my brother's grades could use the extra study session.

Rollins gets up and makes his way back to his bedroom. Almost immediately, he comes right back out with his backpack hanging off one shoulder and heads toward the door. He flips his lucky baseball cap around, pulling it low over his eyes. "I'll be home in a few hours."

What's Rollins up to in that old warehouse? And why so

secretive?

As soon as I hear my brother's car door close in the driveway, I announce I'm full.

My dad glances over at my half-eaten plate of food, before nodding in my direction as well. My mom finishes off her drink in a swallow and reaches for the bottle in the middle of the dinner table, completely ignoring me. I have to get out of here.

As soon as I get back to my room, I go straight for the window, cracking it open. Just as I stick my first leg out the window, I hear my mom yell something muffled at Dad. The windowpane shakes above me, as her shriek reaches a new all-time high. My parents haven't been getting along lately, which is maybe another reason why Dad stays at work so late. I hear glass shatter in the other room, cueing me to slide my other leg over the ledge, before gently closing the window behind me. I jump on my bike with no brakes, and without giving it a second thought, I start peddling downtown as fast as I can and away from my house.

*   *   *

The sun has already set behind me as I near the same building I spotted Rollins entering a couple months back. I spy an aerial drone approaching me, just as I'm propping my bike up against the wall around the corner from what appears to be the only entrance. A ShadowHawk drone slows and almost silently hovers over me for few seconds, maybe fifteen or twenty feet in the air. Its black metallic body is much bigger than a real hawk, about the same size as a small car. I watch a red light flash on, scanning me for my identity. It must be looking for someone. A few seconds later, the red beam clicks off and the drone continues its search down a side street a block away.

I exhale. Even though drones are supposed to make us feel safer, they've always made me nervous. You hear stories about drones coming in the middle of the night and snatching people right out of their own beds. The news rarely covers incidents like those, but people talk—when *they* are not listening.

As I make my way toward the entrance, I hold my stare at the darkening sky, making sure I'm alone. The only working streetlight on the block halfway shines over the warehouse door. Even at night, I can tell the place is a dump. Strips of red and green paint hang down, waving in the breeze, showing the rotten wood exterior underneath. Part of a corner of the roof is roughly flapping back and forth in the wind, exposing the whole right side of the building.

I push on the handle and the door caves in about an inch, releasing an almost noiseless creak. I listen for voices on the other side of the door, but all I can hear is the sound of the loose part of the roof smacking itself against the side of the old building over and over.

"Hey, boy," a raspy voice calls out from behind, making me jump.

Startled, I turn toward an old, battered car parked outside the entrance of the warehouse. The wheel-less vehicle, sitting on four cinder blocks, is full of so many dings and dents, it more resembles a crumpled up piece of paper that someone tried to flatten out than an exterior of a car. The passenger door creaks halfway open, and a man—maybe in his late fifties or early sixties, with long grayish-blond hair and a scraggly beard full of knots steps out and into my long, stretched-out shadow.

"Have you some money, boy?"

The man inches closer, sticking his wrinkled, callused hand out to me, staring into my eyes. Black dirt blankets his face and hands, telling me that he has not bathed in months, probably longer. He squints at me like he's trying to place me, even though we've never met before.

"A kid like you gotta have some parents that pay good money for their boy, yeah?"

I freeze. I still have one hand on the edge of the door, wedging the tips of my fingers farther and farther into the soft, rotting wood that feels more like a sponge now.

"Got anything?" he questions again a little louder, stepping forward, cutting the distance between us in half. His hand is still stretched out toward me, cupped, waiting for money.

He wobbles even closer, spilling out a horrible odor, causing me to take another couple of steps back. My free hand hits the edge of the door, just as my feet get tangled up underneath me. I stumble backward and fall through the partially shut door, finding myself on the dirty floor of the entrance inside the warehouse. I immediately shut the door behind me with a thud, wedging myself up against the only barrier from the menacing homeless man on the other side.

Sweats runs down my forehead, reminding me why I'm here.

4

I look all around…no sign of Rollins.

No sign of anyone.

Weird.

The small warehouse is desolate, except for a couple of piles of old, broken wooden pallets stacked up into two corners of the open space. The lone streetlight from outside provides a low glow, illuminating most of the entrance through the hole in the roof. A closed office door is located in the back of the practically bare room, with a small line of dim light shooting out from underneath, telling me I'm not alone.

"I could watch this a hundred times," a high-pitched voice cries out from behind the closed door, followed by laughter. "Play it again, Liam!"

The laughter propels me off the ground. I release my hold on the door and break into a sprint to the closer of the two corners of the room, diving behind a pile of wooden pallets stacked up underneath the only window in an otherwise windowless building.

The second I am in the corner, the back door flies open. Two teenage boys walk out, followed by a man who looks to be slightly older than them.

"Where is everyone?" the older one exclaims. "You did tell them eight o'clock, right?" The man has olive-colored skin and long, dark hair slicked back. He has on a green military jacket and camouflage pants. He looks like he just went AWOL from the government's army.

"Yes, Victor, we did as you instructed," the dark-skinned boy says, now staring off in my direction, as if something caught his eye.

I dart farther back behind the mound of pallets, even though I know if he saw me, it's already too late. Sitting on the ground, I squeeze my eyes shut, pulling my knees in toward me, trying to make myself into the smallest ball possible.

"Come and get me when the rest of them arrive," I hear the older man bark out, followed by the sound of the back office door slamming shut again.

I keep my eyes closed, listening to the silence for a few seconds, praying I'm alone again. The sound of a pair of boots slowly marching across the warehouse's vinyl floor, heading in my direction, forces me to open my eyes. I look up at a partially opened window above me. There's no way I can fit through the window, even if it was low enough to reach.

The clicking and clacking sound of the approaching boots increases, telling me I'm about to be discovered. I slide around to the other side of the pallet pile, closer to the wall, ready to make a run for the front door. I peek my head around the corner, just in time to see the boy's dark hand grab at the edge of a broken pallet lying on the top of my hiding place.

I hold my breath. What are they going to do once they discover me? All of the worst-case scenarios instantly flood my brain, making the homeless man from earlier seem harmless now.

"Whatcha got over there?" I hear a voice call out from the other end of the warehouse.

"Thought I saw something," the concerned boy answers from only a few feet away from where I cower, still continuing his search.

The front door suddenly opens, pulling my predator away from my corner of the room, at least for the time being. Numerous chattering voices fill the warehouse, telling me there is now a group of at least five or six people on the other side of the pallets.

"It's about time," the deep voice, now moving away from me, bellows toward the group who just entered.

I have to get out of here. What was I thinking? Rollins isn't even here. I look down at my Receiver and see it's a few minutes past eight o'clock. The front door opens up again and more people enter; this group seems to be a larger than the first. I dare to take a quick look around the edge of the pallets, just in time to watch the last boy walk through the entrance. He's wearing a hood over his face, but the brim to a familiar faded, garnet baseball cap sticks out underneath it. *Rollins.* He pushes the door shut and locks it as if he has done this a million times. A click rings out, echoing loudly through the abandoned warehouse.

Following the click, almost like clockwork, the back office door opens up again, forcing me to crawl around to a different hiding spot behind the wooden pallets. From where I sit now, I have a pretty good view of the floor—and of Rollins.

Everyone gathers around the man, the one who the dark-skinned boy called Victor earlier. He's clearly the one in charge.

"We scored big today," Victor begins with a gentle smirk, looking around the small group of followers in front of him. "With the haul we made off with today, we're looking at bigger and better things!"

I count sixteen teenage boys, all who appear to be of high school age, huddled around their leader in a semi-circle, listening intently.

The majority of the attentive group cheers in excitement. Their faces mimic the enthusiasm of their leader as he begins to pace back and forth in front of them in a militaristic way. My eyes flash from one person to the next until they land back on my older brother, Rollins. He's just standing there in the back of the group, showing zero expression, as if he has heard this speech before and knows the outcome.

The man in charge stops in mid-pace and swings back around, acknowledging my brother for the first time.

"And where were you earlier, Rollins?" the man questions, cutting a path through the middle of the group, approaching my brother. "You too good for us now?"

Rollins stares blankly back at him, refusing to let on if he is nervous or not.

The man shifts his attention back toward the rest of the group, as if he cannot fathom one of his followers being disobedient.

"Apparently," he continues, giving up hope on receiving a response from Rollins, "we have a *Tele* in the group who doesn't like to take orders." His voice echoes through the warehouse, stressing the word Tele in a derogatory way, similar to the way the news reporter did earlier about the bank robbery and gas truck explosion.

Wait. Rollins is a Tele? My eyes grow large listening to the man they call Victor.

All in one motion, the group's leader spins back around, away from the group. His arm extends out in front of him, parallel to the ground, lifting an open palm in my brother's direction. Instantly, his telekinetic force takes a hold of Rollins and shoots him across the warehouse floor, slamming him hard up against the wall to my left. The back of his head bounces off the wall on contact and he lolls over on his side on the ground, unconscious.

"I've taught him how to use his gifts and he repays me by hurting the group?" Victor casually spins back around again, away from where Rollins lays comatose, continuing the show for his minions. "When you turn your back on the group—*on the cause*—you stand alone...or in this case"—he curls up his top lip into a sneer—"you sit alone."

No one laughs at the joke. About half of the group takes a step back in fear from their leader, as he inches closer to them.

"Tonight was supposed to be a night of celebration," Victor continues, feeding off the frightened faces before him. "Tonight was supposed to be a night where we all become one." He begins his slow pace again, back and forth in front of the group, taking a step each time the loose part of roof slaps itself against the open part of the building above me.

"Someone could've gotten hurt today," a small voice from the back of the group says, interrupting their leader's victory speech.

Everyone's eyes, including Victor's, find the owner of the small voice in the back.

"Yeah, I didn't sign up for this," a sour-faced boy adds, forcing the unwanted attention all on himself now. "You were supposed to just show us how to control our abilities, not trick us into helping you steal."

"Your gifts!" Victor exclaims, his eyes shifting back and forth between the two Teles who dared to interrupt him. The word *gifts* echoes loudly through the warehouse, somehow setting off a rumble all around us, shaking the walls and the floor underneath me. The stack of wooden pallets in front of me begins to tremble, mirroring the rest of the building.

Frightened, I look up just as the roof over my head begins to peel back, the wind detaching the loose section from the building. A group of five ShadowHawk drones appear, hovering over the now exposed part of the warehouse, filling the room with red beams.

"This is the government," a robotic-sounding voice announces over a loudspeaker. "An illegal telekinetic act has been performed in public. You are all now under arrest. Lie down on the floor and place both of your hands behind your back. This will be your only warning."

The group of followers scatter in different directions, with the majority of them heading for the only exit, leaving a small group of three dark figures making a run for the back office, led by their cowardly leader, Victor.

FootSoldier drones are lowered into the building, armed with automatic weapons, forcing the majority of the teenage Teles to comply with their orders. I watch as a nearby drone slaps a pair of handcuffs around the wrists of an unconscious Rollins, leaving him slumped over on his side with half of his face still against the warehouse floor. The FootSoldier then turns toward me, revealing a mysterious symbol painted across its robotic chest. An image of a large blackbird, with a red star for an eye, stares back at me.

An image that I've seen before, but where? And what does it mean?

CHAPTER 1

PIGGY

"Hey, Piggy…you're not gonna cry, are ya?"

Lukin Meyer forcefully shoves me back into a group of kids gathering behind one of the abandoned classrooms in the rear of our school. Their hands automatically propel me back into the naturally formed circle of kids rooting on what they think will be a quick beat down.

"I'll teach you to snitch," Lukin bellows out loudly over the ever-increasing crowd so that everyone can hear the show he's putting on for them. A long silver chain dangles around his neck, swinging a medallion in the shape of a silver pistol across his broad chest. He's almost a foot taller than me with wide shoulders and an even longer reach. His eyes lock onto mine. He's intentionally squinting, as if the sun is hitting him directly in the face and he can't see me clearly.

"I didn't say nothin'," I mumble back under my breath, so low I'm not even sure if he heard me.

A crooked smile forms across his face. "Well, thanks to you, Piggy, I'm now suspended." Lukin runs his hands through his almost shoulder-length, curly brown hair and pulls it back tight behind his head. A black tattoo of the grim reaper is revealed on the side of his neck. "You know how much business you're costing me, not being allowed on campus?"

I think back to earlier in the day when I entered and then almost immediately exited a smoky boys' bathroom on the second floor of the school—a smoky boys' bathroom that Lukin Meyer and his crew were busily selling drugs out of to students. The Pharmacy is what everyone calls it—a mobile drug store located somewhere new on campus every day. Only Lukin's customers know the location, and no one would ever snitch on him. Everyone knows that.

"Pound 'im!" a smaller kid in a dirty white shirt with the sleeves cut off shouts out over the increasingly rowdy crowd.

I take my eyes off Lukin and glance over at the sleeveless boy squawking at us. I recognize him from earlier at the Pharmacy. He's swaying back and forth on the inner part of the circle, close to Lukin, taunting me. I focus on his eyebrows, which almost forms a point at the bridge of his nose. He has a long, thin scar that runs down his cheek. It starts about an inch or so underneath his left eye before hooking in toward the edge of his mouth. A tattoo of a cross dripping crimson is drawn on his upper arm where his sleeve should be.

"Make him pay, Luke!" A skinny kid shouts out from the other side of the circle.

The crowd responds in a cheer, only to encourage their leader more.

Lukin parades around his circle of friends, laughing, delaying the inevitable. Every few seconds, he jumps toward me. I cower back. I can see the outline of a pack of cigarettes forming a lump in the front pocket of his jeans. Smoking was banned years ago in Sol, but with the kind of money Lukin makes daily, there are ways to still get them.

"You should've never walked into my store today, Piggy," Lukin says. He pauses before taking in a deep breath and switching up the tone in his voice to sound friendlier. "But you did. And then you snitched." He bites at the ring in his bottom lip and inches closer to me. He wears the same scar down the side of his cheek as the sleeveless boy with the knife tattoo, but Lukin's is a little lighter and more faded than the boy's. Must be some form of initiation.

He sticks his index finger out and shoves me hard in the middle of my chest.

I stumble back a few steps before feeling multiple hands behind me forcefully thrust me back into the center of the circle with the big ape.

Lukin glances over at a tall, slender, gothic-looking girl named Winter and gives her a confident wink. I've seen Winter hanging out in the freshman wing before, even though she obviously looks older than me. She pulls back a strand of her long, dark hair and shows off the countless silver earrings and trinkets that fill her ears.

Lukin continues the show for his audience, as he struts back and forth around the circle before deciding he's had enough fun. Without warning, he springs forward and squares his body with mine. He pulls back his massive fist and launches it into my gut.

My mouth tries to force out a low groan, but there's nothing there. I keel over, the wind knocked out of me. I reach for oxygen—oxygen I know was just all around me, but is now gone. I begin choking on the little bit of saliva that sticks to the back of my throat, gasping for even one simple breath of air.

Uncontrollable laughter begins to fill in the circle.

I lift my head and my lungs remember how to work again. I glance over at Winter and watch her saunter out into the center of the circle, her eyes locked onto Lukin's the entire time, as if they are the only two people in the courtyard. She wraps her long arms around his neck and plants a big, wet kiss on his lips. His hand reaches down to just above where her skirt begins and pulls her in closer.

Someone in the crowd yelps out in a mocking tone at the two of them kissing in front of everyone. All of the attention is now on them. They have forgotten all about me—all about the fight. How is that even possible?

I stand there invisible, almost now blending in with the crowd, not knowing what to do. They're gonna stop kissing at some point. I tilt my head back and bellow out a loud, whooping war cry. I charge at the couple from across the circle. With everything I have, I plow into them and send all three of us to the ground on contact.

Winter cries out in horror and shoves me off her. Both of her hands grip to the front of her knee as she screams out in pain. A streak of red is left on the pavement beneath us, along with a thin layer of skin that used to cover the top of her knee.

The entire crowd goes quiet.

Only one word enters my head—*idiot.*

I roll over and push myself to my feet. A sharp pain jolts through my elbow.

"Oh, you've done it now, Piggy," the same sleeveless boy jumps out behind me.

Without saying a word, Lukin pushes himself up and wipes his hands off on the sides of his jeans. He steps forward. His breath smells like road kill, with an odd hint of Winter's cherry lip gloss still on his lips. His crooked smile appears again out of thin air, informing me that I screwed up. Our eyes lock and he pulls me in closer. He doesn't allow me to blink—it's almost as if he has me hypnotized. Lukin pulls back his enormous fist and swings it through the air, connecting with the side of my face.

Bam!

The punch rifles my body back into the same group of hands that just shoved me back in. The strike sends me down to the ground. My eyes water up right away, and my nose begins to throb. A high-pitched ringing fills my head, louder than any air raid drill horn I've ever heard in our sector.

"Get up, Piggy!" It's a kid I don't recognize, standing almost on top of me. "Just imagine he's a giant Twinkie. Get up, Piggy! You know you want it!"

I force my eyes to focus and touch the tip of my nose with my index finger and thumb. It screams back in pain. I think it's broken. I look up and attempt to focus on the voice yelling at me and all I see is black. It's as if I'm wearing an eyepatch—my left eye is swollen shut.

CHAPTER 2

SHADOWHAWK

When I lift myself up off the pavement, my body wobbles back and forth, searching for some kind of inner balance.

"Hey, Piggy," a tan girl with bleach blonde hair and facial piercings yells out with a laugh, "you think you see your trough over there? It's not feeding time yet!"

One of her friends, who looks like she could be her twin, begins making an oinking sound while laughing at her side.

"Oink, oink, oink…"

More kids begin to echo the bleach twins, chiming in with their own mocking piggy sounds.

I shake my head and want to scream.

I watch as Lukin helps Winter off the ground with one hand and walks her over to where the bleach twins continue to giggle. As he turns, his squinty black eyes land on me. The look that he wears tells me he's done playing games.

I swallow hard and search over the bedlam of students who continue to yell at me, encouraging me to fight. My one good eye locks onto a small red car in the near distance as it speeds down the big hill, which runs parallel to the side of the school. The car is all over the road. It dodges other vehicles left and right on both sides of the street. I can just make out the frantic expression on the woman's face as she races past the school. The car is heading straight for the sidewalk at the bottom of the hill where two unknowing young girls are walking in the opposite direction, not paying any attention at all.

An empty feeling of pain shoots through my stomach—the woman has no control over her car.

I dart toward the hill, pushing and shoving my way through the crowd like a mad man—a crowd that continues to grow, even though the fight is now over. Breathing heavily, I come to an abrupt stop not even ten yards away from the road. The red car is rapidly approaching the wall and, in the process, the two little girls. Both girls have on matching pink backpacks, arms draped across each other's shoulders, and are hopping over what are probably the cracks in the sidewalk.

I reach my arm out at about eye level, palm facing toward the street, and focus on the back wheels of the out-of-control car. I clamp my mouth down and grit my teeth. I've never attempted—or moved—any object so large, moving at such a fast speed before. I block out all of the shouting behind me—the curse words, the insults about my weight and concentrate on the car. My brain begins to throb and my swollen eye feels like it's going to explode out of its socket, but just as the car is about to run out of road, it begins to decrease in speed, coming to a rolling stop. The two front tires inch their way onto the sidewalk in front of the wall.

I watch as the woman halfway gets out of the car at the bottom of the hill. "Oh my Lord, you girls okay? My brakes! My brakes wouldn't work!" She wears the same dumfounded look on her face as the crowd behind of me.

The crowd behind me!

I bite down hard on my bottom lip and turn around to face what now feels like the entire school standing there. No one's saying a word. All eyes are on me, all displaying the same bewildered look. About a dozen or so of them have their wrists pointed outward, Receivers directed toward me, filming my show. In the matter of seconds, this will be all over GovtNet.

"Tele," one small boy shouts out, breaking the eerie silence and my train of thought.

I've never heard anyone call me that before. The way the boy said it, he meant it to hurt me.

"He's a Tele!" the small boy repeats, even louder this time, before looking around at everyone for approval.

"He's a Tele!" a girl with short brown hair shouts out, echoing the boy. She stands on the other side of the gathered clump of people who used to resemble a circle.

Slowly, a dark-skinned girl with long braids begins a chant that the rest of the crowd immediately picks up on. "Tel-e...Tel-e...Tel-e..."

The crowd continues chanting, but with each step I take forward, the entire group takes a single step back, including Lukin Meyer, as if I'm a human bomb who's about to detonate.

"Tel-e...Tel-e...Tel-e..."

Behind me, I hear a low, faint humming noise approaching overhead. The Tele chant dies. Everyone's eyes dart away from me and up toward a group of skyscrapers on the other side of the street behind me.

I turn, already knowing what's begetting the sound. A ShadowHawk drone is heading straight toward the school, and I know exactly who they're looking for.

Me.

CHAPTER 3

THE METRO

Everyone scatters in all directions. While the majority of the crowd heads for the front of campus, I race off in the opposite direction toward the skyscrapers—toward the approaching ShadowHawk's low humming noise droning over the sector. I have no choice. With very few trees left in Sol, the only cover I'll have from the Hawk will be from the elevated buildings.

I race across the street, zigzagging around parked vehicles, which have now all stopped on the hill in awe after watching my magic show involving the red car. A group of gray, almost colorless tall buildings, all practically identical and standing next to each other in a single row appear before me. Their huge, powerful shadows blanket the street, absorbing even the slightest bits of light. In the center of it all sits the tallest of the group, the Metro. The building once served as the center for central security for all of Sol and its subsectors, but that was back before the Uprising of the NoMads and the Government being forced to move their security to an undisclosed location.

I look up and spot one of the many security cameras pointing in my direction. It reminds me of how it used to be when that's all they had—the cameras. *No wonder they found me so fast.*

I turn my head to look up the street. Most of the buildings that surround the Metro are similar to these—decrepit and in much need of repair. Mostly brown weeds grow up the sides of the buildings, filling in where cracks and chunks of the foundation have deteriorated over the years. My sector wants nothing to do with these old buildings and treats them like the homeless wandering the streets: it's cheaper just to leave them alone in the condition they're in, so they just stand.

I wipe at the stream of sweat running down the side of my face and place the image of the security camera in the back of my head. Maybe I can cut through the Metro and duck out the other side? It's really my only chance. My one open eye focuses on an already busted-out office window just a few feet in front of me. I feel a presence of a dark cloud beginning to creep over the backside of the building—the aerial drone.

I dive head first through the open hole and tumble awkwardly onto the floor. On my way through, the front of my shirt catches an old nail sticking maybe a quarter of the way out on the inside part of the ledge. I clutch my midsection as if it would crumble into a million pieces if I pull my hand away, before scowling back at the nail in disgust. I needed something to blame for all of this.

Boom!

An explosion goes off in the building next door, courtesy of the ShadowHawk drone flying over. The floor trembles underneath me. Chunks of the old foundation break off from the neighboring structure and crash down into the street behind me.

I peek my head over the open window ledge and watch the drone continue to glide through the air as if it had nothing to do with the recent blast. ShadowHawks have a built-in heat seeker always running when on a mission; it must have picked up something with a pulse next door.

The unmanned aircraft is about thirty feet off the ground. It runs parallel to the street that separates my school from the Metro. I hold my breath as the Hawk passes by the building and somehow leaves me undetected. I have to move, but I can't seem to convince my body to cooperate.

I rest my head against the wall and take in a deep breath. A faint smell of urine enters my nostrils. I hunch my shoulders over, almost in a relaxed state as if this was all over, as if I beat the drone and the peerless Government who runs Sol. I lift the front of my torn shirt and examine my midsection. An oval, about the side of a softball is temporarily tattooed above my bellybutton, compliments of Lukin's fist. It has already turned a dark red, almost purplish color. Self-consciously, I yank my shirt back down. I focus on a covered fat roll bulging through my thin shirt—an imperfection that wasn't there last summer…well, at least one that wasn't so noticeable.

Piggy.

The moniker pops into my head. I *hate* that name.

I think back and can picture every kid's face who has ever called me that. A name I despise more than anything else—a name that's been haunting me all freshman year.

Piggy.

I shake my head in disgust, mad at the world. Mad at my fat stomach bulging out over my waistline.

Boom!

Another explosion goes off a couple of blocks down the street from the Metro, forcing me to stop feeling sorry for myself. I turn my head and look out the busted window using my one open eye. Nothing. The street is quiet following the mayhem, as if I am the last person alive in Sol.

"I can't believe I just did that," I mumble out loud, reliving the recent events in my head. I can't go back to school now. I can't even go home. FootSoldier drones are probably already at my house searching for me. I can picture them questioning my parents on my whereabouts. They'll be stunned when the drones show up. My parents don't even know I'm a Tele—nor did they know about Rollins, either.

Thwok!

Someone kicks at something in the room next to me. My eyes dart toward the closed door on the opposite side of the room that probably used to be an office for some entry-level security expert years ago.

Just a rat, I half-heartily convince myself.

Thwok!

There it goes again. My eyes widen as I watch the door handle begin to turn.

I scour the small office in search of something I can use to block the entrance. The only thing that sits between the door and me is an old wooden desk and a spinning office chair. The desk is missing a front leg, and tilts downward at an angle. I reach my palm out toward the old piece of office furniture and focus. I can feel how heavy it is just as it begins to drag itself across the grubby carpet.

A dark shadow shoots underneath the doorframe and climbs across the floor.

"Who's in there?" a low, muffled voice shouts out from outside of the room. The door peeks open, but only about an inch.

I let go of the desk and flip my palm toward the door. It slams shuts with a thud. I hold the door closed, my hand still extended out in front of me with little difficulty. Just as I'm about to release it, I feel a force pushing—repelling against me—forcing the door back open. Whoever's on the other side is really strong.

The door begins to bulge inward around the edges, leaving only the middle still intact. The top and bottom parts of the door begin to groan, bending inward and then—Bam! The door flies open. It slams itself up against the inside wall and the sound echoes through the small room.

A tall, lanky boy—who couldn't be more than fifteen or sixteen years old—stands with a slight hunch, bewildered, staring back at me in disbelief. A facial tattoo consisting of four vertical red lines begins underneath his chin and runs up to the edge of his bottom lip. Each line is equal in size and width, with the middle two lines centered on either side of his nose. His head is shaven, except for a shoulder-length, bright red, braided ponytail growing out of the back of his head. He has on a torn black T-shirt and jeans, both appearing to be a bit too small on him, like they aren't really his.

A Tele!

The Government has been warning the public about Teles for years. Ever since the Uprising—before the sectors and subsectors were formed and before there was even a need for the Metro. Signs are posted all over Sol about the dangers of interacting with a Tele:

———

They are different. They are not one of us. They cannot be trusted.

———

Is this one of those deranged Teles the Government is always warning the public about?

I stare at the boy, both of us waiting for the other to speak.

"What're you doin' here?" His island accent is thick, but understandable.

I have to force my eyes to make contact with his. "I just screwed up is all…snatched some old lady's purse a couple of blocks down." My eyes shift way. "I just needed a quick score. Ducked in here for a few minutes to hide." A rim of sweat builds across my forehead.

The teenage boy glances off to the side to process what he just heard. He laughs deeply with a smile, yet in short breaths, and looks down at the carpet. His fiery red ponytail falls over the front of his shoulder.

I can't tell if he's buying it.

"What's your name, mate?" The smile is gone, but you can hear a hint of friendliness in his voice.

"Nicholas," I answer, taking a step back.

"What did you really do?" He stares back at me, intense. "They don't send Hawks out for some pursesnatcher." The look in his eyes tell me he knows the answer to his own question before I can answer it, so I ask one of my own.

"Is there a back way outta here?"

Boom!

Before the boy even has a chance to respond, an explosion, followed immediately by an intense bright light goes off somewhere nearby in the building. The blast sends sheets of ceiling and debris raining down all upon us.

CHAPTER 4

RED TRACKER

A chunk of plaster falls and jabs me in the middle of my back as I dive underneath the three-legged desk that sits in the middle of the office floor where I left it. The room fills with the office from above and becomes engulfed in a big white cloud of smoke.

A muffled voice calls out to me in distress.

"You okay?" I shout back, hoping the boy can find my voice amongst all of the chaos.

Only a loud crack resounds, sending more of the ceiling crumbling down all around me. A sharp, jagged piece strikes the carpet inches away from where my foot hides under the desk. I pull my shaking shoe in closer and shut my eyes.

Boom!

Another explosion goes off somewhere in the building, and again the floor rumbles. I feel a large hand grab at my foot, shaking it, forcing my good eye open.

I let out a sigh of relief.

"You alright, mate?" the boy asks, his voice a little shaky. He scoots toward me on his hands and knees. His face is scrunched up, agape, telling me he's probably just as surprised to see me as I am of him.

I slide inward and allow the boy to wedge his body beneath the desk. Another large chunk of plaster breaks off from above and shatters over us on impact.

"That was a close one, yeah?" He pauses, as if he is waiting for my response before glancing back in the direction he just came from. "Someone must really want you bad."

I shake my head and stare off to the side.

"You're a Tele, aren't you?"

I nod once. My eyes shift from the boy to a random pile of debris on the carpet in the corner of the room.

"I knew it." He smiles confidently. "They're not trying to kill you. They're just trying to scare you out. Come on." He nods his head outward, but then turns back. "I'm Kingston, by the way."

He gives me a wink, as if to show that he can be trusted. What other option do I really have? Another chunk of the ceiling falls and strikes the desk. Two large pipes protrude from above and spout out a fountain of water in the opposite corner of the room.

"Follow me." He lowers his voice. "And stay quiet. They've probably already sent the FootSoldiers in."

Kingston gets back on his hands and knees, staying as close as he can to the ground. I follow him through a makeshift tunnel of plaster and wreckage, conveniently leading us in the direction of the door. When we reach the hallway, I look to our left in horror; the first explosion destroyed the entire left side of the building mirroring the room we just exited. Ceilings are caved in and it appears the entire southeastern corner of the Metro has been turned into rubble.

Kingston helps me off the ground and then freezes. He holds one finger to the tip of his ear and points down the hallway. Multiple red, circular beams bounce around against the wall as they signal a group of FootSoldier drones making their way up the opposite hall.

"This way," Kingston whispers. He grabs me by the shirtsleeve and practically drags me down the only other pathway before us. He yanks open a set of unlocked double doors before closing them, putting the little bit of light we had from outside behind us.

*   *   *

A short time later, my guide in front of me halts without warning, as if he has chosen the wrong path and he's now lost. We've reached a dead end after rushing through the confusing maze of dark hallways that make up the Metro. Kingston's eyes wander around the hallway, like a small insect's would, before landing on the ceiling above us in front of a closed office door.

"Give me a lift, mate?" Kingston's stare doesn't leave the ceiling. His eyes study a small air conditioning vent above us. A narrow beam of sunlight slices in from an opened office's window across the hallway, telling me we're near one of the outer walls.

"What's in there?" I ignore Kingston's request.

We'd passed a myriad of opened office doors along the way, all containing whatever was left behind when the Government abandoned the building. This is the first office door we've come across that remains shut.

"Someone left something in there for me. It's important." He turns back. "Trust me."

I study Kingston's face and then glance back at the closed door. Someone had spray painted four vertical white lines, all parallel and equal length, maybe six or seven inches long in the upper right corner of the door. Without taking my eyes off the strange markings, I reach out for the handle and pull it down.

It's locked.

There's a key card reader built into the doorframe, one of those where you swipe your security card and the door opens, but the tiny activation light is not even lit up. Like the rest of the building, the power has been turned off.

"Could've told you it's locked, mate."

Keeping my hand on the metal handle, I turn toward Kingston. I watch as he raises his hand and positions it toward the vent about five or six feet over us. Within seconds, the screws magically pop out and the metal vent falls to the floor between us.

"Don't have a lot of time here," he says, arching his eyebrows. "Wanna give me a hand?"

After only learning about my gift a few months back, I'm still not used to using it openly in front of people, so it takes me a second to respond. I raise my arm and open the palm of my hand, lining it up with Kingston. He begins to rise up into the dark hole as if he's a floating ghost. Without hesitation, Kingston then lifts me up the same way. My head bangs hard on the top of the metal air duct once I'm inside the tiny tunnel. *Great, more crawling.* I rub at the small bump already forming on the top of my head, while keeping my one good eye locked onto the back of Kingston's dirt-stained feet. His words from earlier—*Trust me*—ring loudly through my head. He did save me back there, but what's so important in this room?

A wave of a mixture of mildew and heat hits me at the same time as we begin making our journey into the darkness. Little slits of light shoot out up ahead, maybe ten or twenty yards away from us; it's too dark to tell. As we inch inward, I sense the walls closing in all around me, where it gets to the point that the width of the passageway is narrower than I am wide. I lay my entire body down as flat as I can and use only my forearms to slide—really pull— myself through the dark passageway, almost like a snake or a worm. Each time I pull myself a few inches forward, the entire air duct rattles underneath us.

Bang! Pull. Grunt...

Bang! Pull. Grunt...

Bang! Pull. Grunt...

It's almost rhythmic listening to myself slithering behind the long, lanky Kingston, who seems to have no problem crawling through the tunnel on his hands and knees, as if it's second nature to him.

Gradually, we make it down the dark passageway, before my guide comes to a welcome stop. Kingston points his opened hand toward the air vent beneath him and it drops to the floor. He swings himself around like a circus performer, and leaps down into the hole.

I'm now all alone in the small tunnel. I move closer toward the hole and try to swing my own legs through, mimicking Kingston, only to leave myself hanging down, sticking partially out of the ceiling. The top half of my body feels even more wedged-in than it did before. I lock my fingers around the inside edges of the hole and begin to push myself out of the tiny opening. I have more than half of my body free when I slip and lose my grip. I'm not sure what my original plan was, but this isn't it. I let out a loud yelp and tumble the last few feet down onto the unyielding floor. I twist my body in midair and land on my already aching arm. I roll to the side and clutch my throbbing limb, releasing a long moan. My body feels like it's been put through a ten-round fight today—a fight in which I feel like I got my butt kicked.

Kingston lets out a short, "Shhh..." He sits at a desk in front of an old dinosaur of a computer that he has somehow figured out how to turn on without a conceivable power source. The glowing monitor stares back at him as he reads something off it. Kingston pauses and swivels around in his chair. "You have a death wish, Tele? FootSoldiers are crawling all over the Metro by now." He calls me a Tele in a belittling way, like he's not one himself.

I push myself up in anguish and step up behind where Kingston is sitting in the old office chair. My one good eye focuses on the bright red ponytail that grows out of the back of his head. He has a small, circular scar about the size of a quarter just below where his hairline would begin on the back of his neck.

"A member of the NoMads loaded a virus on here that can put an end to all of this nonsense and shutdown Lee and his program for good," he says, redirecting my eyes away from his scar and back onto the screen. Kingston continues searching the database on the computer, while every few seconds typing in a new command onto the screen.

"The NoMads?" I squeeze out. My voice cracks. "Commander Lee?"

Kingston ignores me and continues to click away at the keys. He sends a series of numbers and letters flying down the screen at a rapid pace. He leans forward and studies the code more closely. I mimic him, as if a giant magnet is pulling us both closer to the screen.

"Wha—" I begin to question, just as a bright red, glowing light abruptly projects outward from the Receiver around my wrist. I freeze. The red glow illuminates the entire office. It grows brighter and brighter before it reaches its limit and recedes into nothing.

Kingston swivels around in his chair, his eyes landing on my wrist in disbelief. The red glow flares up again, but this time for only a second or two before flashing back off again, and then on again, and then off again—continuing the pattern over and over.

I glance up at Kingston and then over to the Receiver around his wrist, but there's nothing there. That's strange. Everyone receives one when they turn seven, and you can't remove it under any circumstances. I think back to the instructions my parents gave me on my seventh birthday.

"You didn't disable your Receiver?" He looks over at my wrist and then up at me, flabbergasted.

I lift my shoulders and stare blankly back at him. This can't be good.

Kingston jumps out of the swivel chair and grabs my wrist. "They've activated your Tracker. They're gonna be here any second!" He presses and holds in a tiny, camouflaged button on the side of the device that I've never noticed before. A small computer chip about a quarter of the size of my pinky nail pops out of the slot. The red flashing light halts. He drops the chip to the ground between us and nods at it.

"Smash it," he says, nodding down.

Without question, I lift up my shoe and bring it back down over the tiny chip, putting it out of its misery.

Kingston whips back around and gets back to work as if the Tracker going off wasn't a big deal at all. He continues to type on the keyboard. Various series of code fills the screen every few seconds that might as well be written in a different language. He hits the ENTER button and the screen goes blank.

"Vent dislodged, Commander." I hear a muffled, computerized voice make their presence known outside the office door behind us. "Request to enter?"

We both turn and stare at the closed door. A long, dark shadow seeps in from underneath.

Kingston pulls out a chip, identical to the one I just smashed and injects it into the computer. "Run." His eyes do not leave the enormous monitor in front of him. "I have to complete my mission."

He lifts out his palm and shoots me back up into the hole above us. I bang my head on the air duct's ceiling in the same spot as before.

"Close the vent," he calls up to me, as I watch him eject the chip from the computer. He pops it into his mouth and swallows. A loud bang, followed by an explosion sends the door open and off its hinges behind him. The effects from the blast leaves the small office in a thick cloud of white smoke.

Three FootSoldiers storm in and grab Kingston before he can even get up out of the chair. One drone spots the broken Tracker chip, along with the loose AC vent, both lying in the center of the floor next to each other.

"Where's the boy?" one FootSoldier says in its computerized voice. The smoke begins to filter out the doorway.

"Boy?" Kingston questions with a smirk across his face. "I don't know of any boy, mate."

I watch from above as Kingston whips his free arm around in the direction of the drone that still has his hand locked onto his shoulder. Just as he turns, another FootSoldier standing at attention in the doorway pulls out his gun and shoots Kingston square in the chest.

Kingston slumps out of the swivel chair and falls to the ground.

CHAPTER 5

TOCSINS

"He's up in the vents."

All three FootSoldiers' gazes shoot up toward the hole in the ceiling, forcing me to recoil farther back into the air duct. A picture of a lifeless Kingston laying on the floor in-between the two drones burns in my mind.

He's dead because of me.

Boom!

A blast from one of the Soldiers' guns below creates a gaping hole in the ceiling only a couple of feet away from where I cower. The explosion shakes and pushes me even farther back into the cramped tunnel we just crawled through. Instead of slithering myself back out toward the hallway—the dead end—I squeeze myself into an even smaller tunnel that opens up to my left.

Boom!

Light shoots out behind me, as the blasts follow me into a new tunnel. The fresh hole illuminates my new passageway, enough for me to see that it widens out ahead. I'm able to get back down onto my hands and knees, stealthily crawling toward…who knows what.

Boom! Boom!

Two more mortars go off at the same time behind me, but I only see a single opening. I pause and stare over my shoulder into the light. The other shot must have been directed toward a different tunnel. That can only mean one thing—they don't know where I am.

"We lost him, Commander." I clearly hear the deep, mechanical voice somewhere below me.

I place my ear against the tunnel floor. There is silence as the FootSoldier waits for further instructions.

"Launch the Tocsins, Soldier."

"Launching the Tocsins, Commander."

Before I even have time to react, four more explosions go off in all directions around me, one after the other.

Boom! Boom! Boom! Boom!

At first there is an ominous silence, but it only lasts for a second at the most. It's overpowered by an immediate silver light illuminating the entire tunnel where I lay helplessly. A piercing, high-pitched ringing follows that takes over the entire air duct. I close my one open eye and attempt to lift my head, but I can't even force myself to do that. A deafening, screeching sound has filled my entire body. I'm paralyzed. I try to lift my head off the tunnel floor again, but it feels like it weighs a thousand pounds.

I force open my eye, and the tunnel is spinning. I see double, triple everything. Move, I order myself. My head lolls to the side, and I can sense my lunch from earlier wanting to make another appearance. My head feels like it's about to implode. I squeeze out a tiny, low groan while still attempting to cup both of my hands over my ears in agony. I lose my balance; my head bangs up against the side of the tunnel wall.

I freeze.

I just gave myself away. The screeching sound begins to recede around me, but I can still feel the vibrations echoing throughout the tunnel. My vision is blurry and I sense my eyes starting to water.

Boom!

Another Tocsin attacks my tunnel behind me. I close my good eye and blindly push forward, trying to block out the deafening siren.

Boom!

The Tocsins are getting closer. They seem to be only concentrating on my tunnel now.

I spot a split in the air duct ahead with two paths that lead in opposite directions. If I choose the wrong one, I may never get out of here.

Boom!

Another Tocsin blasts through the front of the tunnel to the right making the decision easy for me. As I enter the untouched air duct, I turn just in time to watch the entire metal floor behind me detach itself from the ceiling and crumble down on top of the two FootSoldiers underneath it. Chunks of ceiling, along with countless pieces of debris and shrapnel rain down on the Soldiers where they stand. The rubble smothers them to the point I cannot even see them anymore.

Then it hits me. What happened to the third Soldier…and Kingston's body? Did they just leave him back in the office with the computer? I consider retracing my steps to find the office again, but I have no idea where to look, so I shake off the idea.

Even though the threat of the drones is gone, the piercing Tocsins continue to blare through the neighboring tunnels. Since I'm not worried about making noise anymore, I pick up the pace. Just as I come around a turn, I see a vent at the end of the air duct with light slicing through it. Too much light to be coming from inside the building, I convince myself.

I crawl even faster, reaching the dead end and gaze out of the vent onto the street. I note how abnormally quiet everything seems. Empty is a better word for it, there's not a soul in sight. I smell fresh air and spot the once headless statue of Commander Lee erect on the sidewalk, telling me that I've reached the front of the building. The statue was put up to remind the people of Sol of our current, *great* leader. During the Uprising, someone had decapitated it, so the Government closed the Metro down for good. The statue was rebuilt following the Metro move.

I reach out my palm and detach the air vent within seconds. It orbits down onto the sidewalk below. I poke my head out and look up at the sky—no Hawks. The sun shines back overhead; at last, something's going my way. At the end of my tunnel, it really opens up so I have enough room to maneuver my legs around and jump out of the building.

Not even a second after my feet hit the ground, a cluster of FootSoldier drones swarm around me. I turn back toward the vent. It's too high to reach. I turn and face the organized group of drones all huddled around me in a semi-circle. All of them are wearing protective Tele shells, an invention Commander Lee is credited with creating, so I couldn't use my telekinetic powers against them even if I wanted to.

I lift both of my hands, signaling I will go peacefully. One FootSoldier approaches me and lowers its gun. The drone then pulls out a pair of handcuffs, ready to slap them on me. I can't go out like this. What would my brother Rollins say? My eyes dart all around the semi-circle with only the Metro to my back. I shoot up my hand and aim it toward the neck of one of the drones—the only part not covered by the shell.

Another Soldier to my right senses my strike and fires.

Everything goes black.

CHAPTER 6

COCKPIT

I'm not sure how long I was out, but when I wake, my mouth tastes chalky dry. I can now open both eyes, but all I see is a reflection of myself staring back at me in a sea of black. A steel helmet is encased around my entire head, reminding me of a biker's helmet that you can't see through. There's a mouthguard lodged between my teeth, which prevents me from talking. My hands and legs are tightly fastened on either side of my seat; I'm paralyzed. The only functional parts that are not secure are my ears, so I listen...

The muffled, rumbling hum of an engine fills the room where I sit as a prisoner in my own body. An image of a plane immediately flashes in my brain. In a panic, I try to jerk my head around, forcefully attempting to move even an inch, but whatever holds me down refuses to give. Instead, I let out a silent groan in its place. I'm locked in.

"It's okay, son. This will all be a distant memory to you soon," an unrecognizable, deep voice informs me, cutting through the rumble of the engine. The man places his hand on my shoulder and pats it a couple of times in an almost comforting way.

I've been caught. And it's all because of one thing—the video.

The whole reason why I'm even here is because of the video. Was it posted just yesterday? The day before? A week ago? It feels so long ago since the Metro—since the fight—but at the same time it feels like it could've happened earlier in the day. It really doesn't matter now, though. Either way I broke my one rule and was caught.

And now I'm here on a plane in complete darkness—destination unknown.

I sense the man next to me rise out of his seat. "I have one who's awake," he calls out to someone. Like everything else, his voice is then swallowed up by the rumble of what sounds like a plane's engine.

Moments later, I sense us suddenly jerk down in what feels like an unexpected dip in altitude. A loud alarm shrieks out and overpowers the drone of the engine. It's a different tone than the deafening blasts of the Tocsins; this sounds more like a warning.

"We have a problem," someone calls out in distress, possibly a woman, as the high-pitched voice rushes past me. Running, the person trips over the side of my paralyzed foot and falls to the floor. A loud boom goes off behind me that forces the plane into an immediate nosedive.

The woman grabs a hold of my knee to steady herself. Not being strapped down in a seat, she's having difficulty catching her balance.

Boom!

Another blast goes off in front of us. The rate of the klaxon increases. I can picture a red flashing light accompanying the loud siren that fills the aircraft.

"We're going down!" a shaky voice calls out, confirming my thoughts of being on a plane.

My seat is vibrating at such a rapid rate I can actually move my feet a little bit now. I sense multiple people rushing around me, attempting to secure themselves for impact. The plane jerks up and sends a body flying across the open space in front of me, followed by a loud crack. The plane's nose begins to teeter back and forth in an attempt to gain some form of control.

"We've lost part of the wing!" I hear someone shout out in a panic. "We're under attack!"

Boom!

Another strike hits us—the entire plane drops, only to lift back up again, sending us into a tailspin. The useless warning siren continues to blare as I feel items fly past my feet. Something solid smacks me right in the head, but whatever it is, it bounces off my mask and is shot outward.

We make contact with something and then the plane freezes. The alarm shuts off and everything seems eerily still. I listen for voices around me, but no one's making a sound. I try to jerk my head around again and, surprisingly, this time my neck's free. I attempt to lift up my arms and move my feet, and they're both free, too. I hear a loud suction sound and the device around my face comes loose. I lift up on the contraption and it slides off my head.

I look around. There are four others, all still strapped into their seats surrounding me. Two are seated across the open aisle that separates us, and the other two are secured on either side of where I sit. There's a woman dressed in all black lying motionless on her stomach in an awkward position up against the wall in the back of the plane. Dark red blood oozes from her forehead above her left eye. The man, who I assume is the same man trying to comfort me earlier, lies unconscious on the floor between the two others and me. He's dressed in the same matching dark gear as the woman in the rear of the plane. A large wooden pallet full of canned vegetables lies on top of him.

Am I the only survivor?

I push myself out of the seat and my legs feel like rubber. I grimace as I put my full weight on them. Without even taking a step, I can feel the floorboard underneath tremble a bit.

"Help!" I hear a deep, muffled boy's voice scream out in terror. It's coming from one of the passengers seated across from me. "Is there anyone there?"

And then, one by one, the other seated passengers begin crying out for help to one another. None of them seem to be free, but are able to communicate.

"I'm over here," yells one from the direction of the first boy screaming out.

"Please, help me!" the first boy answers.

I stand still, going back and forth between the two conscious prisoners locked in their seats. I take a step toward the two voices, and the entire floorboard teeters in the opposite direction. The nose of the plane tilts downward and causes the tail to lift up. It feels like I'm on one of those giant seesaw rides on a playground. If I move too fast in either direction, the unsteady plane will fall. I take a step back and the aircraft shifts to its original position again. I reach out and grab hold of the rail behind me to steady myself.

"Help! I can't move!"

My eyes dart over my shoulder toward the panicky voice—a

girl's voice. She's sitting two empty seats down from me toward the tail of the plane. Still gripping the wall behind me, I begin to lower myself down the small incline until I reach the girl. I try to yank off her helmet with one hand, while still gripping onto the rail above her head. The mask will not budge. I hold out my free hand, palm out, and try prying it off that way. Still nothing. There has to be some kind of control switch around here. My eyes dart all around the cabin and land on the cockpit door, labeled PILOT.

"I'll be right back." I want her to know I really do plan on returning.

"Wait, wait, wait," she calls out. "Don't leave me!"

I ignore her plea, but I can hear her choking back tears in her voice as she continues to call out for me in terror.

"Please, don't leave me!"

I picture tears running down her cheeks, underneath her mask, lost in what's going on here.

I begin to pull myself up the incline with both hands and grip onto the rail that leads all the way to the front. Rows of empty seats on either side of the plane run parallel to each other, making up the inner walls of the aircraft. Between the two rows of seats is empty space, probably used to store cargo.

Every time I take a step, no matter how small it is, I can feel the plane move. The sound of metal creaks with every careful step I take, vibrating the floorboard underneath me. I pause and let out a loud exhale. I look back over my shoulder at the surreal reminder of the woman lying dead in the rear of the plane. I don't want to end up like her.

I continue my climb up to the front and reach for the cockpit door. I can't seem to talk myself into letting go of the railing attached to the inner wall. I extend my fingers out toward the handle a little bit more, but it's just out of reach. I lean my weight back against the wall and raise my arm again. Almost instantly, the cockpit door flies open, and the copilot shoots out toward the tail of the plane. The copilot's body smashes up against the rear of the aircraft, right above where the lifeless woman lays. The entire plane shifts weight the opposite way. I jump toward the open door handle and pull myself into the cockpit in hopes of rebalancing the weight in the plane. The aircraft teeters back again, leveling out, just as I close the door

CHAPTER 7

COMPASS

I begin to scour over the plane's instrument panel made up of about a thousand different buttons, levers, and knobs—all labeled in some kind of unidentifiable code. Each button is marked with a single digit number, followed by a capital letter.

The floor hiccups below me and forces me to catch myself on the back of the pilot's chair. I look down at the motionless man sitting in front of me; he's still loosely strapped into his seat. His entire body is leaning forward, his head resting on the instrument panel in front of him. He bears the tattoo of a blackbird on the back of his neck in the same spot as Kingston's scar. His eyes are closed as if he is just knocked unconscious, appearing peaceful.

I pull back on the pilot's shoulder and lift him off the controls. A shallow puddle of blood is left in his place. Both of his eyes remain closed, but I discover a jagged piece of steel broken off from a lever sticking about a half an inch out of his forehead, just above his right eye. The ghostly look on the man's face causes me to jump back, and in result, shift the front of the plane down a few inches. I tighten my grip on the edge of the pilot's seat and look out the window in front of me for the first time since entering the cockpit.

I'm awestruck. An ocean of green treetops blankets out in front of me as far as I can see. I release my hold on the seat. I've never seen anything like it. To see a small group of live trees in Sol today is a rarity, this place is an anomaly. A fiery red and orange sun sets high in the west, just over the imaginary line where the vast forest must end. I've seen the sun set hundreds of times before, but it's never looked like this. For the first time since probably before Rollins was taken, a smile forms across my face, and I allow my mind to go blank. I forget about everything: the survivors in the cabin...the drones...the Government...that I'm a Tele—and for a brief moment, I feel like a normal kid growing up in a different part of the world.

Skrawww! Skrawww!

A bizarre-looking white bird with a long, wide orange beak flies by the window of the cockpit and shrieks at me. It immediately snaps me out of my selfish daze. The bird appears to be a mix of a whooping crane and a mallard duck.

Skrawww! Skrawww!

The annoyingly loud bird lands on the nose of the plane, lifts up one of its two skinny legs in the air and scratches its back feathers with its talon. The front of the plane inches downward and disrupts the bird's new resting spot, making it fly off. The plane shifts back, and teeters a couple of times before settling again. I realize now we could fall to our deaths at any moment. I have to find that release button.

I continue my search over the panel for a couple more minutes before deciding to just start hitting random buttons. The first button I choose turns on a bright light over the copilot's seat. The next button turns on a motor, which silences itself after a few seconds. I shake my head in frustration and look around. The syrupy pool of the pilot's blood on the control panel draws me in. There is a series of bloodstained buttons, each labeled with a single digit staring back at me. Only four of the buttons are still lit up. I push in the first one and the red bulb above it disappears. I push in the second button, only to duplicate the first result. I glance back at the cabin and listen for voices.

Nothing.

I push in the final two buttons at the same time and release them. The instrument panel is now dark.

Thwok!

Something ricochets off the outer part of the cockpit door behind me. I freeze and swing my head around toward the noise.

"Help!" I hear a muffled voice cry out from the other side of the door.

I reach out and pull down on the handle—it's locked. I push hard on the door and shove my weight into it, but it doesn't budge. I take a couple of steps back and hold out my hand, aiming it just left of the handle. I can feel the weight of the door trying to give on the other side; the top of the frame bends outward, but it holds strong. I'm stuck.

I turn back around and face my possible demise—the instrument panel. Maybe there's a release button for the door, too? My eyes scurry over the massive board searching for something to free me. The longer I stay in the cabin, the more I can sense the nose of the plane teetering over. I have to get out of here.

My eyes fly around the cockpit and land on a single dim, glowing red bulb blinking on and off on the far corner of the panel—almost covered by the lifeless pilot's hand. I sidestep around the backside of his chair and keep my eyes glued to the red blinking bulb in front of me, as if it will shut off if I look away. I extend out my hand and use my telekinetic force to push in the lone button. The cockpit door shoots open behind me and smacks itself against the outer wall of the cabin. The sound of the banging door echoes throughout the plane, announcing my location.

My eyes study the gaping hole of a doorway for a moment. I wait for cries of help or even the sound of someone stirring, but there's nothing. A loud crack from the tree limb below fills the cockpit, murdering the unnatural silence. I back away from the pilot's chair and inch my way toward the cabin.

I poke my head through the open door and note all of the seats but one is empty. A single masked person remains motionless, still imprisoned. I take a step into the cabin and I'm welcomed with a dynamic kick that strikes the side of my face just under my chin.

Bam!

A invisible wave of telekinetic force knocks me back a few feet. My head smacks up against the bottom edge of the instrument panel behind me. The nose of the plane jerks down another foot, causing yet another loud crack beneath the floorboard.

I shake myself and search for clarity. My entire head feels like it was just struck by a charging rhino going full speed. I sit motionless, stunned, and lean my head back on the control panel, confused on how I got here. A dark shadow interrupts my thoughts and casts itself through the cockpit doorway over where I lay. A short teenage girl appears and steps forward. Her presence reminds me of how I ended up on the ground with my head spinning. She stands in the doorframe leaning to the side, and looks down at me in a judgmental way. Her short, bleached blonde hair is the color of the sun with a strand of pink hanging down over her right eye. A tattoo of a blue nautical compass pointing to the south is drawn on the top of her hand. She's dressed in all white, just like me, and wears a deadly smirk across her alluring face.

"Name and rank," she utters, breaking her own silence. She straightens up her pose, almost self-consciously. She holds no weapon, but her eyes tell me she's the reason I'm lying on the ground.

I begin to push myself up off the floorboard, which puts the girl into a ready martial arts stance in front of me.

I release myself and slump back down. "Nicholas," I mumble, giving in. I pull my knees up toward my chin, which results in a sharp sting in the middle of my stomach. "I'm from Sol. No rank."

She takes another small step forward; the nose of the plane teeters slightly downward.

"Stop!" I shout out in full panic mode. "Look out the window!" And then, as if on cue, the branch below us cries out in a loud crack, releasing its hold on the entire plane.

CHAPTER 8

HUNTING KNIFE

The plane drops another five or ten feet before the next limb down catches us, cracking loudly upon impact. The girl has to catch herself against the narrow walls to keep from losing her balance. Her eyes shoot from the cockpit window to me and then back out the window. "I'm Ria," she says in a shaky voice. Her eyes gaze back out the large window behind me. "You a Tele, too?"

I nod. "When we crashed, I was released by him." I motion back at the pilot slumped over in his seat. "I think his head hit my release button when he fell forward." I rub at my sore chin. "How did you do that anyway?"

Ria shrugs. "Been able to bend air since I turned twelve." She delicately pulls back a strand of her pink bangs and hooks it behind her ear, only for it to fall right back into place over her eye. Two cowardly looking teenage boys appear behind her, staring at me through the open cockpit door.

"Can we trust him?" the bigger of the two asks no one in particular.

"He's one of us," Ria answers confidently, as if she was certain the boy was questioning her. "This is August." She introduces the bigger of the two teens who stand behind her in the doorway.

August lumbers out and has to duck his head as he enters the cockpit. The plane vibrates with each big step taken. He's tall, a good six inches taller than me and at least a foot taller than Ria. He has shaggy, light brown hair and a short, dark beard of stubble dotted across his face. His upper arm muscles bulge out of the same white outfit we all wear. He sports a blank expression on his face, nowhere near ready to hand over his trust to me yet.

"And this is Ren." Ria finishes her short introductions with a genuine smile.

A timid, olive-skinned, slightly younger-looking boy steps out from behind Ria's shadow. The size of the boy tells me he can't be older than eleven or twelve. He refuses to make eye contact with me, keeping his eyes glued to the back of Ria's boots.

"Well, it's really great to meet everyone," I begin sarcastically, "but we need to get off this plane—*now!*" A loud crack shoots up through the floorboards and echoes off the walls in the small cockpit. Ria and August look out the window behind me.

"There's someone still in there," Ren squeaks out. He takes a small step back from the group. "We couldn't wake him." He turns to face the cabin.

"We don't have time," August bellows. He turns back and eyes the exit hatch. "Maybe he didn't even survive the crash?" He looks over at Ria and waits to see if she agrees with him. It's obvious he has feelings for her.

Ria ignores August and glances back at the masked person, making her move toward him. Ren and I follow. The nose of the plane begins to lift itself up the farther we all move inward. We sidestep around the unconscious soldier still lying in the middle of the floor underneath the mound of cans. Everyone's eyes glance down at the fallen man on his back as we pass by without saying a word.

"Suit yourselves," August mutters. The tone of his voice reveals his feelings are hurt. He slumps off in the direction of the only exit and begins to work on opening the latch.

The lone masked prisoner sits upright and motionless, just mere feet away from the soldier on the floor covered in cans of vegetables. We crowd around the seat and form a semi-circle, no one really knowing what to do. Ria leans forward and checks his pulse to see if he is even still alive. She nods her head. Wanting to help, I step forward and examine the mask where it's attached to the stainless steel wall behind the seat.

Click!

August unlatches the heavy steel door and it creaks outward. The entire plane shifts downward, nose up, causing a gradual slide toward the tail end. August turns back and shakes his head at us before leaping out of the hole. He lands safely on a strong branch of a neighboring tree. "Come on, Ria. Jump! You're gonna get yourself killed!"

With the sudden change in balance, the nose of the small aircraft lifts up a few more feet. The three of us tumble onto the floor and slide backward toward the tail. I reach out and blindly grab a hold of a steel bar running parallel to the floor, the only thing preventing me from sliding. Ria grabs my free hand, and Ren wraps himself around her leg. A stampede of loose cans comes charging at us and ricochets hard off the back wall. The plane continues its incline, ready to send us over the edge at any second.

Bam!

There's a loud thud in front of me, which ends the decline of the plane. I look up and discover August standing in a crouched position a few feet away, holding onto the same rail as I am. He stretches out his free hand inches away from mine. I reach out and lock hands with him, letting go of the rail. With a single grunt, August yanks all three of us up toward him and attempts to even out the balance of the aircraft.

Ria lifts herself up, along with Ren, and then the four of us point our palms toward the masked prisoner. We all concentrate on one thing—the release of the helmet. Together we pull until we hear a loud pop. The headgear slides off and falls to our feet. A neon red, braided ponytail falls out and snakes itself over the unconscious teen's shoulder.

Kingston!

Without asking permission, August grabs a hold of Ria and throws her over his shoulder. He looks back at me and Ren and says with a sneer, "I'm not leaving without her this time," before jumping out of the opening. He lands on the same tree branch as he did before.

The nose of the plane rises up with the sudden change of weight, sending the plane back to its original position. With no time to think, I unlatch Kingston from his seat and, within seconds, send him flying out through the open hatch to safety on the tree limb. I lift up Ren the same way August just picked up Ria and step toward the opening. Just as I'm about to jump, I glance back at the soldier lying unconscious in the middle of the cabin floor. On his belt is a long, black hunting knife in a sheath. It looks identical to a knife I've seen so many times before hanging off my older brother's waist. I freeze and force myself to take a small step back. Even though I can sense the plane freefalling over the edge at any moment, I turn toward the motionless soldier and hold out my hand. Frightened, Ren tightens his grip around my neck as the knife flies the short distance across the cabin and into my open palm. I steal a quick glance down at the weapon and read back the initials *R.M.* engraved into the butt of the handle—initials I already knew were there.

Rollins McCready.

I wrap my fingers around my brother's knife, before leaping out of the hatch with Ren still in my arms. The tree releases its hold on the plane allowing the aircraft to plummet, tail end first, crashing below us in a small fiery explosion.

CHAPTER 9

MUD

"We're not taking him with us," August clamors, again looking over at Ria for acceptance. "He's just gonna slow us down." He spits to the side, as if to give his command an explanation point.

No one says a word, including Ria, which tells me she's not going to leave Kingston out in the middle of a strange forest.

"I know him," I halfheartedly confess to the group. I hold a hard stare and look down at a curled up Kingston at our feet. I can feel everyone else's eyes on me waiting for me to continue. "His name's Kingston. If it wasn't for..." I begin, before deciding to keep some things a secret. "We're both from Sol." I glance up, choosing to make eye contact with Ria first, I guess for acceptance as well, before diverting my eyes away from the group and toward the fire still flickering to our backs.

"We need to get a move on," Ria announces, taking charge. "And he *is* coming with us." She directs the second half of her response toward August, who responds with an eye roll and sucking in his teeth. Without even being told, August slumps over and lifts up Kingston with an impudent groan. Kingston's red ponytail falls over August's bulging biceps and forearms.

"Wait!" Ren shouts out. His worried stare shoots all around us. "You hear that?"

We halt, our eyes following Ren's gaze.

"I don't hear nothin'," August spouts, not even trying to listen. He glances over at Ria. "You really goin' along with these two losers?"

Ria holds up her hand with a stern look and muzzles August. She continues her search across the darkening sky, canopied with tall, green treetops hanging down all around us. "I think I hear something, too."

We hear a low buzzing sound at a distance, alerting us of our attacker. "Drone!" Ren shouts out in a high-pitch voice. He points blindly toward the treetops.

We bolt in the opposite direction, dodging and jumping over countless low-hanging limbs and undergrowth in our way. We follow what appears to be a once man-made trail that has not been used in quite some time. Large, black roots pop up every few feet, crisscrossing over our path in front of us.

"They're gonna be on us any second," August says between breaths. He still holds onto Kingston as his body flaps around in his arms. August's bulging forearms stick out and bounce off low tree limbs blocking the path as he brings up the rear. The low humming noise behind us increases with each step we take in the opposite direction.

"Over here," Ria shouts. She leads the way and sprints straight into a large coffee-colored pond where our trail ends. Ren and I splash in after her without question. The murky water is dark as tar and almost as thick. It reeks of rotten eggs being left outside on a warm afternoon.

A few yards in, I stumble and lose my balance. I tumble down a sudden drop-off into the deeper end of the pond. I bob down into the water with my eyes open—everything is pitch-black, but I swear I can see tiny black bugs swimming all around me. I bring my head back up to the surface and take in a deep breath, before pulling myself back down to eye level. I spot a group of three ShadowHawk drones approaching the pond from just over a set of low treetops. In a panic, I duck back down underwater. I can feel Ren's petite, bony fingers pulling at my leg, begging to resurface, but I shove him back down even farther. I've lost track of everyone else, but I know they're here somewhere.

Moments later, the water above my head begins to spin lightly, increasing its speed by the second. One of the Hawks is hovering right over me. A feel a small bubble beginning to grow in the middle of my throat, my body's way of telling me it needs oxygen. I force myself to hold out a little longer. The tiny air bubble expands, enticing me to go to the surface.

Just one little breath of air—I try to convince myself that's all I need—just one little breath. I close my eyes and feel my body drift to the surface while letting go of the top of Ren's squirming head. I can sense my body moving closer and closer to the top.

I raise my arms over my head and kick once with my legs, ready to give up. The tiny air bubble escapes my lungs and rises to the surface before exploding over me like a firecracker. A painful, burning sensation replaces the escaped air bubble in my lungs. I stretch out my fingers and reach for the surface, almost feeling the heat from the drone still hovering over us on the other side. I don't care anymore. I kick again to push myself up even farther when I feel a weak set of fingers grab a hold of my ankle and yank me back down to the bottom of the dark pond. I picture the Grim Reaper's cold, bony hand reaching out and pulling me down to him. *Is this what death feels like?*

The spinning of the water above me begins to dissipate...the signal for us to come up. I kick faintly a couple of times and pull myself away from the pond floor, breaking through the surface. I try sucking in a deep breath of air, but in return, bucketfuls of murky, smelly pond water spews out of my lungs instead. Small waves lap back and forth, holding my vomit in front of me for a few seconds before drifting away and sinking. I take in a deep breath of air and the smell of rotten eggs singes the inside of my nose, but I don't care; the air has never felt so good.

"That was close," Ria exclaims. She holds out her arms to help her float next to me. "Wait; where's Ren?"

I spin around in a circle and search for a sign of the boy who saved me from giving myself up to the Hawk. "He was just here!"

"Can he even swim?" Ria questions, uncertain.

"Survival of the fittest," August responds, already ready to abandon the search. He trudges toward the edge of the pond in the same direction that we all just entered moments ago and disappears into a group of tall bushes where he stashed away an unconscious Kingston. Mud covers Kingston from head to toe.

No one says a word. The murky, black water continues to lap back and forth as Ria and I wade into the shallow end of the pond.

"Well"—August turns—"are you two just gonna sit there or—" A big, black glob of goop flies through the air and smacks August right in the mouth, silencing him in mid-sentence. He freezes in disgust before choking and spitting out the putrid black goop that fills the inside of his mouth. "What the—"

"Survival of the fittest, indeed," Ren shouts out in his high-pitched voice. He pops up a few yards away from me in the water with another handful of pond mud already aimed at August on the bank. He lets his second mud bomb fly and connects again with the enemy—this time smacking August on the side of the head.

"You are so dead, little man!" He wipes the muck out of his ear canal and flings it back in Ren's direction.

Ren dives back under the water, laughing, and dodges the attack. August charges out into the pond in the direction of Ren's splash, but again, Ren has disappeared. He pops up on the other side of Ria, and she gives him a small kiss on the cheek. August turns toward Ren, firing a mud bomb of his own, only to smack Ria across the side of her face.

"Oh, now you've done it," Ria shouts. She reaches down and grabs a clump of mud and, with a grin, flings it over in my direction. She makes an explosion noise out of the corner of her mouth, shouting, "We have a hit!"

We all begin laughing—even August cracks a smile for once—and then it hits me, the mud bomb *feels* cool. "That's why the Hawk couldn't detect us," I say, interrupting the fun. "It's because of the mud. It cooled down our body temperature. That's why they missed Kingston too."

I dive back down under the surface, gather up a big clump of the dark, lumpy mud and hold it in toward my stomach like it's buried treasure, before shooting back up toward the surface. I pull myself into the shallow end and lumber out to the bank. I begin spreading the rancid, cool, dark mud all over my body. I start with my face and move all the way down to my boots. By the time I'm finished, there's not an inch of me not covered in the black goop.

"It's like camouflage," Ria says. She joins me on the bank. Without warning, she begins to spread a thick layer of mud across the back of my neck and then moves down my back. A quick jolt shoots through my skin, sending an instant chill over my entire body.

"Think you can help me out with my back, Ria?" August interrupts with a hint of jealously, still standing in the shallow end of the pond. "I'm the one doing all of the hard work here"—he pauses––"carrying around *your* new friend." He looks over at me peevishly, warning me to back off.

"Give me a second." Ria sounds almost annoyed at his request, as she continues to rub cool mud all over my back, noticeably in areas that were already fully covered.

CHAPTER 10

RED NEON LIGHTS

A sharp beam of light slices though the darkening forest and puts an end to our mud party, forcing us to cower behind a fallen tree next to the pond. Thanks to the mud, our bodies are camouflaged, which hides us from the two teenage boys scouring the area after the aerial drones could not detect us.

Both boys are dressed in all black and standing upright, shoulders back. They demonstrate perfect posture. "Well, if the plane went down here, they can't be far," the larger of the two boys says. He points the flashlight in our direction. His hair is cut short, almost buzzed, matching his partner's.

"Who are they?" I whisper to Ria, who appears to be holding her breath. August looks over at me in disgust before shifting to Ria. Ren crouches down by the tree, between us. He holds one hand firmly around Ria's ankle for assurance.

"When they get closer, we have to take them out." August's big, dark eyes stare through us, thinking only one thing—survival.

Out of the corner of my eye, I watch as Ria agrees. She nods in August's direction, which causes his attention to shift back toward me, waiting for my response.

I wrap my fingers nervously around the top of the hunting knife. "We don't know anything about them," I stammer, holding my voice down. "They could be stranded just like us."

August glances down at the knife in my hand and then back up at me. "They could also be working for the people who brought us here...or maybe even who shot down the plane." He pauses and peers out at the two solider-like teens quietly discussing something with each other. Their backs are now facing us, walking in the opposite direction toward the plane wreck. Two singular, circular red neon lights shoot out of the center of each of their necks splitting a path through the night air toward us.

"Still think they're like us?" August asks gruffly. He holds his stare on the two little trails of neon glowing back at us.

The red light is the same color as Kingston's ponytail. It reminds me of the small circular scar I spotted on his neck back at the Metro, along with the pilot's tattoo. "They're Teles," I say confidently. "I don't know why they're looking for us or even how they know we're out here, but they're Teles."

Ren unmasks his face for the first time, sensing it's safe, but still holds his grip around Ria's ankle. His tiny brown eyes flash up at the three of us, tired and homesick. His mouth remains closed.

"Well, if it's just gonna be me and Ria, then so be it." August begins to push himself up. Again, he eyes the hunting knife at my waist. Ria grabs his hand and pulls him back down.

"What're you gonna do? Just walk up and bash them in the heads?"

August's gaze wanders off and it looks like he is trying to form a plan in his head.

"You heard Nic," she says, not letting go of his hand. "They're Teles. Plus they have guns."

I peek my head up over the rotting tree's side and focus on a pair of large guns loosely hanging around their necks. *Why would Teles need guns?*

August shakes Ria's hand away and pulls himself all the way up. "If you three are afraid, just say so." He hops over the tree's side and, without saying another word, jumps behind a set of two larger trees a few feet inward, contemplating his next move.

Ria pulls a strand of hair caked with fresh mud back behind her ear. She does it in an almost flirtatious way, making me forget all about August and the two Teles for a half a second.

"I can't stand when he gets like this."

And as simple as that, she brings me back to the present.

Ria's eyes attempt to follow August into the forest, but I can tell she's already lost sight of him. "August is my ex," she confesses.

"We broke up the same day we both were arrested."

I nod my head. Why is she telling me this? She doesn't owe me an explanation.

"I just know he's going to do something stu—" Ria stops in midsentence. Her eyes spy her ex-boyfriend again, as she watches him creep out into the small clearing that separates us from the two intruders.

I follow her gaze and spot August standing in the clearing, palm out. He faces one of the two boys dressed in black. The other boy searches around the outskirts of the plane fire.

"Stay here with Ren and Kingston." I reach down to pick up a small log sitting by my feet. I wrap my fingers around the end of it and hold my new homemade club across my chest before stumbling over the side of the fallen tree—trying to emulate August's recent limber exit toward the clearing.

In front of me, I watch as August strikes the smaller of the two Teles from behind using telekinesis. He sends the boy flying off into the direction of a group of overgrown bushes on the other side of the wreck. He doesn't even wait for the boy to land; August drops his shoulders and rifles off in a sprint across the clearing.

The airborne Tele crash lands off to the side with a loud thump, causing his partner to jump and drop his flashlight. Shaken, the boy bends down to pick up his light just in time to absorb the backside blow of August's bull charge, which sends them both to the ground in a knot.

Out of breath, I reach them rolling around in the dirt, both struggling to get the upper hand in the wrestling match. The Tele soldier wildly throws a punch through the air and connects with the side of August's large head with a pop. The move gives the boy enough leverage to roll over on top of August. He clamps his hands around his throat and begins choking him.

Even in the darkness, I can see the life fading from August's face. His brown eyes begin to go milky white, matching his paling face. He spews out a gagging sound and locks his large fingers around the Tele's hands, trying to pry them loose from around his neck. His legs shake violently, kicking and digging into the grass.

I have to do something. I have to do something. I have to do something!

I stand wide-eyed over them, the adrenaline pumping through my veins. I remember the club still in my hand and tighten my grip around the end of it. I have to do something, I tell myself again. I stare through the back of the Tele's head. I close my eyes and swing the club, connecting with the back of the boy's skull. He loses his grip and falls unconscious to the side, off August.

"Go grab the other dude's gun," August chokes out, trying to catch his breath. He nods off in the direction of the bushes and pushes himself up. "He should be out." His breath is short, but I can hear the anger in his voice. "I'll take care of this one."

My fingers drop the club, which I now picture with a dark red stain on it, and I rush over to the smaller Tele lying in the bushes. He's sprawled out on his neck, positioned in a way one's neck should never bend. As I'm unhooking the gun from around his shoulders, I notice his red neon light has ceased, almost as if it was his power source. I throw the gun strap over my shoulder and turn back around toward the fire—toward August.

August is hovering over the unconscious boy, wearing a hollow look in his eyes. He has both of his massive arms wrapped around the Tele's thick neck, almost in a headlock position. The boy's eyes are rolled back in his head, but his red neon light continues to shine off the front of August's mud-covered white pants. I inch another small step forward before halting again. I watch as August takes the boy's head and jerks it to the side. A loud crack echoes out into the dark forest, disguising itself as a crack of thunder overhead.

I freeze.

The boy's light extinguishes itself.

August just killed a Tele. A teenage boy.

His guilty eyes glance up at me as he releases the boy, allowing him to fall limply at his feet. "Looks like you got him pretty good there on the back of the head," he says with a deep sigh. "I don't think he'll be giving us any more trouble tonight."

Even though it's dark, I swear I can see a small smirk form across August's face before he replaces it with his usual scowl. He then unhooks the gun from around the boy's neck and leaves him lying dead by the fire.

"Come on. Let's move."

CHAPTER 11

FIRST KILL

I awake the next morning with a low, loud grumble echoing out from deep down in my stomach. The first thing I focus on is the mud smeared across my arms, refreshing my memory of the night before. I'm pressed up against the inner wall of a cave we discovered about a mile or so away from the pond. I roll over, and a sharp rock jabs me in the ribs, making me wince. I glance over at Ria, who I remember falling asleep alone the night before, but who is now nestled between August's brawny, mud-coated arms. Did she *ask* him to cuddle up with her or did August do it on his own? Either way, the sight of them lying there together gives me a strange, sick feeling in the pit of my stomach, forcing me to get up.

I push myself up off the hard ground and feel every rock I slept on last night. A still unconscious, mud-covered Kingston sits close by, propped up against the inner wall of the cave next to where Ria and August still sleep. Hot coals from the remains of a fire we built the night before—thanks to the burning plane—sits close by, helping to shield us from the countless mosquitoes in the forest that have already feasted on us.

I lumber out of our dim shelter, still a little groggy—almost tripping over Ren, who's still lying fast asleep on the floor of the cave. His little chest rises and falls peacefully, reminding me of my older brother Rollins who used to share a bedroom with me when we were younger, years before he was taken.

I walk out into the canopied forest that surrounds the cave and I hear numerous birds calling to one another, but none seem to be in sight. Hunger pains keep gnawing away at my stomach, begging for some breakfast. I think back to the large pallet of canned vegetables spewed across the plane's floor before being destroyed in the fire. I wish I had grabbed even just one can. I pick up a long, skinny stick off the ground and sit on the edge of a fallen tree right outside of the cave, trying to get my mind off food. I pull out my brother's hunting knife and begin sharpening the end of the stick. By time I have a razor-sharp point, I hear August and Ria starting to stir behind me. I pretend not to hear them, but I can clearly make out August's deep, low voice.

"I could lay here all day with you," he says, his face nuzzled up to Ria's ear.

Ria makes a stretching sound of her own and begins to wake up. "What do you think you're doing, August?" She keeps her voice down, not wanting to wake up Ren, but I can sense a smile in her tone.

"You looked cold last night, so I joined you."

I turn around in time to make eye contact with Ria, just as she's lifting her head. She gently pushes a shirtless August away from her in a teasing way, before flashing a bemused look in my direction, as if she doesn't know how he got there.

August takes the hint and grabs his shirt off the ground and storms out of the cave past me without saying a word. I watch as he plods around a large tree, allowing the overgrown forest to swallow him whole. I think back to the look he wore last night after killing the Tele; how easily August just snapped the solder's neck as if the boy wasn't a human being at all.

As soon as August is out of sight, Ria comes out and joins me on the log. "How did you sleep?" Her voice cracks as she says this, still some sleep leftover in her voice from the night before. She shoos away an annoying mosquito.

"Like sleeping on a bed of nails," I halfheartedly answer. I keep my eyes focused on the point at the end of my stick. My stomach bellows out another rumble, loud enough for Ria to hear, but she doesn't react.

"What you saw in there..." she begins, trying to explain herself. "The three of us all come from the same sector—Iris." I can feel her eyes moving up from my hands to my face. "August is just protective over me, that's all."

I don't answer her. Why should I? It's none of my business. I keep my eyes on the end of the stick, rubbing the tip over and over again against the inner edge of my thumb until it starts to feel numb.

"Why don't you go help August?" Ria changes the subject after I refuse to talk. She glances back down at my hands. "I think he went looking for food."

I open my mouth to say something, but then quickly close it and clench my teeth. I nod and push myself off the fallen tree with a grunt, before wandering off in the same direction as August.

*   *   *

I almost immediately catch up with August, who is crouching down behind a large tree. He's staring off in the direction of a brown animal with white spots that has antlers like a deer, but a much smaller body. Its two tiny ears stay erect on either side of its face, as if it's always frightened. The paltry animal is leaning down and nibbling at an overgrown bush about fifteen or so yards away. I clear my throat and make my presence known, causing August to jump.

"What's wrong with you?" His facial expression tells me he wants me here as much as I want to be here.

We both turn to see the small deer-looking animal fire its head in our direction. It stares right through us with its big black eyes. Its nose twitches a little, almost as if it was about to sneeze.

August and I freeze. The small deer holds its stare for a few seconds before turning back toward the ground and, feeling safe once again, continuing its breakfast.

"What're you doin' out here?" he whispers low. August pulls himself up behind the monstrous tree in front of us. He looks down at the stick in my hand and then over to my hunting knife hooked around my belt.

"Figured you could use my help," I say between breaths. Standing next to August, for the first time I truly realize how big he is.

He rolls his eyes. "You really think I need *your* help?" An arrogant smile forms across his face. "Whatcha got there, a spear?"

I glance up and notice one of the guns we pulled off the Teles last night strapped across his burly chest. I nod and look back up, making eye contact with him. My heart's racing. It feels like it's about to jump out of my chest any second.

August looks back down at the hunting knife around my waist.

"You think you can hit that deer with your spear?" He looks out at the miniature animal and then back up at me. He wears the same arrogant expression.

"I know I can," I declare fearlessly, refusing to look away. *Where's this coming from?* I've never thrown a football in gym class before, let alone a spear. When you're homeschooled until the eighth grade, you don't get too many chances to show off your athletic skills at home to your mom.

"You seem confident." August scratches at his chin, caressing the week's growth of stubble across his face. "Let's bet that knife there around your belt." His eyes break away from mine, keeping his smirk in place. "First person to make a kill gets the knife."

I should've known. My eyes dart down to the initials engraved into the top of the handle staring back up at me—*R.M.* I look back up and find August's eyes. "I'll put up the knife, as long as you promise to never leave Kingston behind. I owe him."

"What's up with that kid, anyway?" August steps back and a stick breaks under his big boot. The small deer jumps, quickly swinging its head back in our direction again. Its glassy, onyx eyes search for its hunter, but the large tree does a great job of concealing us.

After almost a full minute, the feeble-minded animal loses interest and inches itself forward, nibbling on a fresh patch of green grass.

"I'll even give you this first one, but you better not scare it off, Doughboy." He pokes at my gut and forces me back. I regain my grip around the middle of the spear and step up to the large tree. The animal has since moved in a little closer to us, no more than ten yards away now, maybe even closer. I lift my spear to eye level and pull it slightly back behind my ear. I take in a deep breath.

"Now or never..."

I wait for August to call me *the* name. I can picture his lips pursing together, forming the first letters of the word—

Piggy.

But he doesn't. I'm not that person out here. I can make a new name for myself, and it all starts with this first kill. I take in another deep breath and ignore August's chatter in my ear about how I'm going to screw this up. I count to three in my head—*one...two...three*—and then take a sizable step forward and around the tree, releasing the spear.

The spear flies a whole five feet in front of me before falling to the ground. The small deer-like animal has had enough scares for one morning; the sudden noise causes it to scamper away, deep into the forest.

August falls to his knees laughing uncontrollably and holds his stomach as if he's in pain. "That was the funniest thing," he spits out between laughs, "I've ever seen. You throw like a girl!" August continues the banter for a few more minutes before he begins wiping away at the tears in his eyes. "You might as well hand over that knife now, Chubs. Save us both some trouble. I can make a quick kill with that fine weapon. We'll be feasting within the hour."

August stands there confidently, arms crossed, waiting for a response I refuse to give him.

Fuming, I pick the spear up from the ground and trudge off alone in the same direction the small deer just dashed off in.

*   *   *

I continue beating myself up as I walk deeper into the forest, not coming across another living thing along my path. I don't want to stray too far away from camp, even though I refuse to come back without some kind of food for everyone.

I wipe away a thick layer of sweat mixed with caked mud off my forehead, while smacking away a group of mosquitos buzzing around my ear with the same hand. The hot sun, acting more like a blowtorch now, shoots through the branches of a huge tree that towers over me. It's early and it is already blazing hot. My legs ache, forcing me to stop to take a break. The back of my throat pinches and begs me for a sip of water. I'm so thirsty the murky pond water from last night would even be welcomed now.

Whoosh...

My ears perk up, sensing something darting through the bushes in my direction. I jump and grab a hold of a low tree limb above my head as the animal comes barreling into my sights. I swing my legs around and pull myself up to safety; the aggressive beast just missing the heel of my boot. Its short, stocky legs can't stop its own momentum in time, injecting itself into the base of the trunk, almost uprooting the tree in one strong motion. The fearless animal's white tusks cut into the hard bark, forcing it to yank and twist its stuck head free from the tree.

Its thick coat of forest green fur matches its surroundings, creating the perfect camouflage for its predators. The beast backs up few steps and aims its boar-like head toward the tree again before striking almost the exact same spot as before.

The tree trembles as if it's sitting on a fault line and a small earthquake shakes underneath us.

Grrrr…

The beast stares up at me, snarling like a dog. I realize now this thing is not going to just grow tired and leave me alone.

The animal backs up again and mimics its first two attacks, trying to shake me loose from my limb. A large dead branch falls from above and slices its way down to the bottom, striking me hard across the top of my head and shoulder. Slipping, my leg swings down, again enticing the beast with the side of boot. I drop my spear and hit the beast across its back. I pull myself back up, nervously clutching the base of the tree branch again.

Grrrr…

The boar-like beast snarls at me again from below. It wears a confident look across its ugly face like it knows I dropped my weapon.

I peer down at the strange animal as it stares up in the tree, almost like it's studying me, trying to learn my habits. "I am going to kill you," I say low under my breath, as if I didn't even believe it myself.

The animal snorts a couple of times, laughing at me from below.

"I'm gonna kill you!" I shout out a little louder, still halfway trying to convince myself. I raise my hands above my head and yell out at the top of my lungs, "I'm gonna—"

The beast, taking full advantage of the situation, emulates its first three attacks and charges the tree. Upon impact, I slip off my branch and tumble hard to the ground. I try to catch myself, but the powerful animal is already on top of me. Its long, white and yellow-stained tusks dig into my ribs, causing me to wince in pain.

I wrestle the beast off me, enough to where I can extend my arm out in front of me for a few seconds. Using my force, I send the confused thing flying off in the opposite direction, blasting it about five feet away into the side of neighboring tree. The animal's head bounces off the hard trunk and it releases a small cry. It flips itself over and comes at me again. I pull out my knife just as the beast launches itself at me and stick it underneath its two front legs. Crimson blood splatters back, covering the front of my shirt with the animal's insides.

The creature continues to flop around, still halfway on top of me, while I try to get a better hold of it. I manage to pull out the knife and jab at it a second and third time under its belly, forcing it to stop moving. A pool of blood forms underneath us. It's over. Exhausted, I release the heavy beast, rolling it off me.

I stare down at the boar-like animal who just tried to kill me and a single thought crosses my mind—*Am I really all that different from August?*

I use the bottom of my already dirty shirt to wipe the fresh blood spatter off my face. I already know the answer.

It doesn't matter. I won.

CHAPTER 12

THE COMPOUND

I walk heavily to the top of a hill that overlooks my kill zone and peer out in all directions. I have the beast's carcass hanging off my shoulders, presenting it to the world as if it's my trophy, but there's no one around to admire it.

The sun continues to beam down on me as if it's shinning through a large magnifying glass. I shoo away a couple of annoying flies that have latched onto me since I started toting the dead animal around on my back. I'm grateful the mosquitoes have left me alone, at least for the time being. I pull down on the animal's hooves resting around my neck and get a better a grip on its stubby legs. I turn back around just in time to catch a glimpse of someone moving off in the distance. *August*. He's hiking off in the opposite direction of our camp, and he's animal-less. I guess I really did win the bet.

Just as I am about to call out to him, August ducks and crouches low behind a large oak tree about fifty yards away. I look all around thinking maybe he sees an animal that he's tracking, but there's nothing there.

I keep my distance, jumping from one tree to the next, quietly hunting my new prey. That's the good and bad about this place— there are plenty of hiding spots for those who do not want to be seen.

August continues his hunt, hiking up a large hill, twice the size of the one I was on earlier before dipping behind a group of scattered trees and bushes. I peek around the corner of the tree that I'm hiding behind and search for him, but he's gone.

He had to have seen me.

I hide for a few more minutes behind the tree before sneaking another look around it again; still no sign of August. The weight of the animal carcass hanging down from around my shoulders pulls on my neck, begging me to unload it. The annoying flies are back, having seemed to have picked up our strong scent. I feel one land on the side of my neck. It leaves an immediate piercing sting in its place before I can slap it away.

I sense a small bump forming, taking the place of the stinger. A warm, sleepy feeling rushes through my body and I lose my balance, stumbling back. I can feel my fingers releasing the beast from around my shoulders as if it's nothing—instead of a trophy I was so proud of only minutes ago.

The carcass drops and lands in a messy pile at my feet. I can sense my knees wanting to follow, buckling underneath me. I attempt to grip onto the tree in front of me, but instead I end up forcing my upper body against the trunk in order to stay upright. My fingertips dig into the rough bark, while my feet scramble underneath me. I struggle for some kind of stability. I can feel the muscles in my fingers beginning to tense up, pulling the weight of my body backward, falling. My head smacks the ground, burying the whole right side of my face into the mud. I'm paralyzed. Another one of those annoying flies circles my limp face and lands on the side of my nose that is visible. I wait for it to plant its tiny, poisonous stinger into me, but it just inches around the side of my face before flying off. I try to fight the warm sensation taking control of my body, but it feels so good.

A dark shadow grows over me, instructing me to go to sleep. And then everything goes dark.

*   *   *

When I wake, I'm all alone. I lay sprawled out across a small cot, my body takes up the entire mattress. The cot is placed in one of the four corners in a small room. The room is not much bigger than the length of the cot, itself—maybe eight by ten feet? A single lamp glows overhead in an almost soothing way. It's not bright, yet it's not too dim. Cold, frigid air is being pumped out of the air conditioning vent positioned right over the bed, forcing me to pull up the blanket all the way up to my chin.

Were we saved?

I don't realize until I place my foot out onto the chilly, tiled floor that all of my clothes are missing, except my underwear. An open closet door on the other side of the room tells me there are clean clothes waiting for me—a long sleeve white T-shirt, white pants, and black polished boots lined up next to each other.

My body appears to have been cleaned, just like my clothes. No longer am I covered in the dark, foul-smelling mud from the pond— once, my camouflage. I swing my other foot out from underneath the warm covers and place it next my other one. The cold sting of the floor surprises me with a zap. I push myself up off the cot and hear a sound mimicking the screams of a thousand different mice being tortured underneath me. I scoot across the tiny room and begin getting dressed.

As I'm sliding my head through the neck hole of the new shirt, I sense the door open behind me. I jump and turn around, but the door remains shut. I scuttle back across the cold floor with only my head through the neck hole and my underwear on, checking the knob.

It's locked.

Confused, I gingerly make my way back across the tiled floor and finish getting dressed. I sit on the cot and release the screams from underneath me again—screams loud enough to convince me to lower my head under the cot to explore the sound.

Nothing.

I look up in the corner of the room and, for the first time, notice a little red dot blinking back at me. *They've been watching me this whole time?*

The tiny, red bulb continues its steady pattern of blinks before speeding up and altering its pattern right before my eyes— blink...blink...pause...blink...blink...pause...

I rub at my eyes. They have to be playing tricks on me; this can't be real. The door handle jiggles again, pulling my eyes off the red blinking light and over toward the knob. The knob begins to spin counterclockwise, slowly at first, but then speeds up—until suddenly it halts, spinning back in the opposite direction before coming to an abrupt stop.

I jump off the cot, the boots still lying on the chilled floor close to the head of the small bed. I grab for the doorknob and this time it turns. I poke my head out and peer down a long, serpentine hallway lit every few yards by a small lamp that almost seems pointless it's so dim.

I scratch at the side of my neck and can feel a small bump that reminds me of the sting in the woods. What was I doing out there in the first place?

August.

I was following August—and then I lost him on the hill.

I jump back onto the cot and slip my feet into my new boots, leaving them untied. The cold air blows down on the back of my neck reminding me of the little red blinking light again. I glance up and then hear the door slam shut. I jump and turn toward the sound; the door is now wide open.

I rub at my eyes again, feeling itchy all over. I'm scared.

I force myself up off the cot, which, once again, creates that horrible rodent-screeching sound. It echoes around me as I step out the door.

*   *   *

I creep down the dim hallway and hug the inside part of the wall, as if I step too far out, I would fall off an imaginary ledge. Streaks of all the different colors of the rainbow beam out in fuzzy rays of light shooting out from the lamps on the wall, leading me down the long, winding corridor. I concentrate on the echo of my boots clicking and clacking off the brick floor, almost in a rhythmic beat—the only thing propelling me down the hallway.

Click...

Clack...

Click...

Clack...

I continue until my ears tell me to freeze. I hear another set of footsteps marching my way, coming from the opposite direction. Instinctively, I reach for my brother's hunting knife from my belt, but it's not there. My trembling hand falls to the side. More trails of light. I lift my hand up in front of my face. It looks different. I see double, maybe triple of my hand waving back and forth, but at the same time, I see my one, single hand clearer than ever before—every wrinkle, every freckle, every blemish clearly highlighted in front of me.

Silence.

I'm alone again.

I focus back on the lights and soon hear the rhythmic sound of my boots clicking and clacking off the bricks below me once more.

*   *   *

I've been walking for… I'm not sure how long. I glance down at my wrist, and like my knife, my Receiver is now also missing. I lift my eyes back up and the trail of rainbows has ended. A large red door in front of me shoots out yellow rays of light from all around it. This is the first door I've come across since coming out of… I turn my head and focus on the hallway wall curving inward. It blinds me from seeing anything more than ten yards back.

I try the doorknob and it turns. I peek my head in, and the room appears to be oddly similar to the one I was in before. My feet walk through the doorway, and the steel door instantly shuts behind me. I glance over toward the closet and two plastic hangers dangle from the bar, both still gently swaying back and forth. My eyes snap over to the small cot in the corner of the room, and I focus on how the sheets are pulled back and how someone's imprint is still an indention on the outer edge of the blanket.

Am I back in the same room? How is that even possible?

I sit back down on the cot, triggering that awful noise once again, and I pull my legs back under the blanket. I feel a stab of fear in the middle of my chest. I'm scared and so tired. I know I need to keep going, but…I could check the door again? But what's the point? The hallway only leads back to this one room. None of this makes any sense to me, but at the same time, it makes complete sense.

As soon as I close my eyes, the lock on the door clicks. I shoot the upper half of body up, and the light overhead immediately shuts off with a heavy thud. I am now surrounded by complete darkness.

CHAPTER 13

RECRUIT

Bam!

Something smacks against the glass window over my head. I bolt up and stretch my neck, looking back over my shoulder.

Nothing.

My eyes drift down discovering a large blackbird—possibly a raven or a crow—lying dead on the ground on the other side of the windowpane.

This all feels too familiar.

Bam!

Another large blackbird mimics the first one, flying kamikaze-style straight into the glass, this time right in front of my eyes. I jump on impact, not expecting it to happen twice. Both birds lie dead next to each other; their dark red, starred eyes beaming back up at me.

Wait...there's not a window in this room.

I blink my eyes and force myself to wake up.

It was all a dream.

The door in front of my cot shoots open and sends the room's overhead lamp on. The light seems brighter today. I squint at the two hazy figures standing back, halfway hidden in the shadows of the doorway. One of the teenage boys, maybe fifteen or sixteen years old, marches into the room as if with a purpose, immediately standing over me.

"Time to go," the hovering teen commands. His muscles bulge

out of his shirt, similar to August, but not quite as intimidating. The boy stands at attention only inches away from the cot. His facial expression tells me that he's waiting for me to respond. He holds a large gun around his neck with his index finger massaging the trigger button. He wears an all black uniform, identical to the Teles in the forest, as does the other boy standing behind him. The boy hovering over me has the name Woodham sewn across his top left shirt pocket, blocked out in all white letters.

I push myself off the cot and slide my feet into my boots. As soon as I stand, Woodham grabs at my elbow and pulls me to the door. A neon red light shoots out of the back of his neck and reflects off the wall behind me where I just imagined the window and the dead blackbirds lying outside. The other boy, still standing in the doorframe and named Dreadnought, shoves the barrel tip of his gun into the side of my already sore ribs, even as he instructs me to not try anything. His red light shines as strong as his partner's.

Teles.

The hallway looks different now. There are no streaks of color coming out of the lamps, nor is there even a steep ledge to my left now. Lamps are located on either side of us illuminating enough to convince me we are in a different hallway than the one yesterday. Single images of a blackbird with a red star for an eye—identical to the tattoo I saw on the back of the pilot's neck—line the walls, located a few inches over each lamp. Everything appears brand new, as if someone had just come in and given the walls a fresh coat of paint. Our passageway curves and winds around the farther we walk away from the room, but just when I expect us to end back up at the red door again, the hallway splits into two, with my guards taking the passageway to our left without hesitation.

We march down another tunnel before coming to a dead end and an opened elevator waiting for us. We enter and the doors automatically close. They form the same painted blackbird symbol before us as the doors come together. There are no floor buttons to select from on the inside of the elevator, but a small keypad is there in its place. The bigger of the two Teles rapidly enters a series of numbers and letters into the keypad, sending us in motion. At first I can't tell if we are moving up or down, but as the elevator comes to a sudden stop, I sense we've dropped several levels.

"Where are you taking me?"

I turn my head toward the Tele on my left, Dreadnought, who forcefully keeps the tip of his gun into my side. He still refuses to make eye contact with me. His partner holds a stare at his own reflection bouncing off the closed steel doors in front of us. Both boys wear a single, small red patch on their left sleeve illustrating the same blackbird with a red star for an eye. The night Rollins was taken comes rushing back to me—the first time I laid eyes on this strange symbol—the same mark the FootSoldier drones proudly displayed across their chests. But what does it mean?

The doors open, and we begin to pick up the pace. We move more briskly down another set of corridors before coming to a short flight of stairs. I can see the bottom of the staircase before I even set foot on the first step. The stairs lead to a closed door, again painted in all red, with no sign or hint of what is waiting on the other side.

The staircase is too narrow for both of the guards to stand on either side of me like before, so Dreadnought falls in behind. He allows Woodham to take the lead. They do this without communicating, as if they've done this numerous times before.

"What's on the other side?"

I know I'm talking to a wall, but the closer we get to the bottom step, the faster my heart beats. I can feel the pit of my stomach beginning to churn. It begs me not to find out what is on the other side of the red door.

The guard leading the way stops as we reach the bottom floor. His red light glows even brighter underneath the staircase. The bright light bounces back off my chest. I look over his shoulder and notice there's no handle on the door.

The guard from behind tightens his grip around my elbow. I can feel his heavy, rhythmic breathing on the back of my neck, almost as if he is sleeping. The lightbulb overhead cuts out. Neither guard flinches. I can hear people shouting on the other side of the red door, signaling a fight or struggle in the next room.

I begin to weigh my options, and walking through the red door is not one of them. Only one of the two guards has a hold on me now— the one standing in the rear.

The guard in front of me holds the edge of a handheld white card against the side of the door, where the handle should be, and I hear a click. *It's now or never.* I flip my elbow back and catch the guard standing behind me right underneath his chin, knocking him off balance. He slips and falls backward. The back of his head strikes the edge of the bottom step and his red light instantly extinguishes.

I bull rush over the Tele's limp body and fly up the stairs. I push myself to run faster than ever before. I know I've got a jump on the guard in front of me, but by not very much. Any second now, I'll be caught.

I turn my head slightly over my shoulder and it appears I'm all alone. I slow down to a jog just as the hall curves to the right and dead ends into a closed elevator. Out of breath, I look around the small area; there's nowhere to go. I hear the elevator doors beginning to open in front of me, so I turn back toward my reflection. I look up, and the little white camera hanging over the elevator doors blinks back. They're watching me.

The doors open and three guards, all armed, immediately aim their automatic weapons toward my chest, forcing me to comply. I throw my hands up in the air and fall to my knees.

"I give up," I mumble, feeling defeated. "You win." I look up with a frown at the small video camera continuously recording me, then my gaze falls to the ground in front of me.

Two of the three guards stomp out of the elevator and hook their forearms underneath my armpits, dragging me in, as the third guard keeps his gun pointed at me the entire time. Once we're in, the doors close and one of the guards fastens a steel helmet around my head, similar to the headgear that imprisoned me on the plane. At first everything is dark until one of the guards presses a button on the rear of the device and the visor goes clear.

I think I sense the elevator climbing, telling me they're taking me to a different place than before. Maybe back to my room? At this point, even that would be comforting.

The elevator doors open, and I'm pulled back out the same way I entered—dragged out on my butt. We move across the hall, and I hear a loud click. I can hear yelling again all around me as if I'm at some kind of sporting event. I'm pulled out onto the floor, where my helmet is removed without warning. I'm all alone.

I look back over my shoulder just in time to watch the three guards exit through a door behind me, before it closes. I lift myself up off the cold floor and scan my surroundings. A spotlight flies around the room, bouncing off the walls and floors. I can't tell how large the room is, but as my eyes begin to follow the spotlight around, I begin making out people's eyes glaring back at me through the darkness. Then their mouths come into view—yelling all sorts of curse words and derogatory phrases at me like I'm some kind of criminal about to be hung in the public square.

An older kid shouts out something muffled and pounds his fists on the transparent plastic barrier in front of him—the only thing separating me from the savage crowd.

Everyone in the building cheers as a song starts up on the loudspeaker, cutting like a knife through the chaos surrounding me. The spectators in the first few rows begin to bang on the plastic barrier to the beat of the heavy metal song being blasted out of the huge speakers that I cannot seem to find. I watch as the crowd simultaneously begins to bob their heads to the beat, each making a fist and thrusting it in the air.

"Ladies and gentlemen…" A voice comes on the loudspeaker, interrupting the flow of the song. "We have a special treat for you tonight!"

The crowd continues to pump their fists to the beat of the music, really feeling it. They begin chanting something, but it's quickly drowned out by the voice on the loudspeaker.

"Normally we'd match this young recruit up against another of his ability, but he tested off the charts!" The announcer pauses for dramatic effect and allows the cheering to continue. "Battling for the first time in the arena—Recruit Nicholas McCready."

Recruit?

I spin around, as a chorus of boos echo down from the bleachers all around me.

The song ends and a new one begins, cueing the door across the hall to begin sliding up into the ceiling. The opening bass line from the song makes my arm hairs stand up. The glow of a neon red light sneaks out as the door rises. A long, stretchy shadow shoots out across the floor, its owner to follow.

"His opponent—" the announcer begins, before the rest of his statement is drowned out by the eruption of noise from the crowd.

My eyes widen as I stare in the direction of the figure standing in the open door frame. It's too dark to make out any of his features, but as soon as our eyes lock, I know who it is I have to battle.

Kingston.

CHAPTER 14

THE ARENA

Kingston inches toward me just as a single large lamp clicks on overhead illuminating only the floor around us. No lights are turned on in the stands, but a neon red glow begins to mushroom, filling the inside of the arena. Only the first ten or so rows are visible from where I stand, but the ever-increasing glow tells me there's not an open seat in the building.

My opponent's entrance music ends, forcing Kingston to walk a few more steps out to me in the center. His eyes are laced with darkness, his stare meeting my gaze for the first time since entering the arena. He stands up straight, as if at attention, tense. A bright neon light shines out of the back of his neck, where the scar once was.

My eyes shoot around the bowl-shaped building. Kingston was recruiting me for *this?* What is this place?

And then it hits me—something I learned in school. This place is like the Roman Coliseum. In Roman times, a king would order convicted criminals and gladiators to fight ferocious beasts, such as a lion or tiger to their death. Kingston is my lion, and I'm his gladiator…or is it the other way around? At least in Roman times, they would give the criminals a weapon to help defend themselves.

Maybe there's something here I can use.

I scan the floor all around me. Various objects lay in the four corners of the room—an old beat-up mattress rests close by, leaning up against the nearest corner to where I stand, along with a cot frame that probably once held the mattress. I can't make out what's underneath them, but off to the side I spot a metal crate tipped over spilling out multiple sealed glass jars filled with some kind of mysterious neon red liquid.

The crowd continues their rhythmic pounding on the transparent barrier surrounding the arena, begging their gladiator to make the first move. Kingston takes a couple of small steps forward and an echoing roar throughout the building fills in any holes of silence that still remain.

My eyes dart over to the adjacent corner in the room, behind where my opponent stands. Smaller objects are stacked up in a pile, including an old microwave, a fire extinguisher, and what looks like a partial set of broken golf clubs.

As if suddenly activated, Kingston whips out his palm and fires a crowbar at me from behind. I duck as the blurred object buzzes over the top of my head. Off target, the crowbar ricochets off the wall on the other side of the room. The crowd grumbles in disappointment, most shifting back in their seats.

"Don't make me do this," Kingston calls out to me with his island accent. He breaks his stare for a few seconds. His eyes tell me he remembers me, but behind his glossy gaze I see a look of terror.

I have to do something or I'm dead.

Kingston's red ponytail flips to the side as he turns his head toward the crowd. He raises a single closed fist in the air, a signal for power.

The arena erupts.

I steal a quick glance at the blind corner behind me, from where the crowbar just took flight. A large flat screen television remains flipped upside down next to a small stack of old books. I jerk my hand up and send the television flying across the arena floor. The spotlight follows it sailing through the air, giving Kingston all the warning he needs to block it.

My opponent waits until the last possible second to flip his hand up and regain control over the television. I instantly feel how powerful Kingston is.

The crowd cheers with excitement.

"Don't make...me...do...this!" Kingston pleads, screaming out again, this time in short bursts, almost as if it's painful for him to say it. His eyes scan the room, still holding the flat screen between us with ease.

Sweat trickles down my face as I widen my stance. *Don't make him do what?*

Kingston inches toward me; with each step he takes, the television mirrors him as if it's a boomerang slowly returning to my hand. My left eye begins to pulsate, sending a sharp, unbearable, shooting pain through my head.

I cringe and drop my arm, releasing my hold on the monitor in midair.

The unrestricted television strikes me across my forearm and shoulder, sideswiping me across the face. The force knocks me to the ground and leaves the whole right side of my body numb. A gash almost the length of my entire arm opens up as I lay still. Blood gushes down the side of my forehead. I close my eyes, the pain telling me to throw in the towel.

I can picture Kingston looking me over—studying me—not yet satisfied with the damage he has done. He's rubbing his knuckles back and forth, switching from left to the right, salivating at a chance to continue the fight. The crowd continues to cheer for their champion, not yet ready to end the day's entertainment.

Shuttering, my one visible eye barely peeks open just as Kingston levitates me off the ground. I fly backward, slamming back first against the barrier ten feet behind me. My skull thumps hard against the wall. An invisible hand holds me up by the neck a few feet off the ground while choking the life out of me. The powerful force burns through my neck like a taut rope. I try opening my mouth to beg him to stop, but nothing comes out. My legs are furiously pumping, trying to find the ground as I bang my fists against the wall behind me over and over again, gasping for a single breath of air.

Then, all of a sudden, he releases me. I slump to the ground, choking, attempting to suck in the much-needed oxygen. I steal a quick glance over at Kingston and weakly slide myself away from him, from the wall. His arms are hanging to his side and he's staring up into the dark of the audience. The crowd responds in another roar, everyone jumping out of their seats.

I push myself painfully up off the hard floor. As Kingston turns, I bull rush toward him and launch myself into his midsection. He flips up his arm late just as I strike him. Easily outweighing him, I knock him to the ground and smash the side of his face into the floor.

Shoving both hands into the side of his head, I nervously glance around for something to use as a weapon. The broken flat screen lays somewhere behind me, but I don't see it.

I halfway turn and allow Kingston just enough leverage to spin himself around, knocking me off him. He grabs my forehead and slams the back of my head down on the floor.

"I don't wanna do this," he mumbles down at me. This time I'm only the one who can hear him. His hands are still wrapped around my head, shoving my face farther and farther down into the ground.

Dazed, I try pushing him off me, but I realize this is an impossible feat. It feels like I have a cloud lingering in my head. I can't think straight. I turn to the side and search for the flat screen one more time—my only chance of survival. My vision is blurred, but I'm certain it's not here. I search the floor for another weapon. One of the mysterious red jars from across the room catches my eye. I spin around and send the jar rocketing through the air.

Smack!

"Ahhhh!" he screams out in horror. The red liquid burns a hole through his skin as if it's acid. The glass jar has made contact with the side of Kingston's face, mere inches away from his eye. He falls to the side, cupping his face with both hands.

I spin myself around and find the flat screen. There are several large cracks down the middle of it where it struck me before. With everything I have left, I lift up the television and shoot it over in Kingston's direction as he gets to his knees.

The TV strikes him across the back of his head with a sickening crunch, extinguishing his red light. Kingston keels over onto his knees before the top half of his lanky frame crumbles down like an old, abandoned building.

It's over.

I wobble over to him. Kingston's sprawled across the arena floor. Dark red blood runs out of his ear and out of a large gash on the side of his face. A small pool of maroon forms around him.

I turn away, ashamed.

My arms fall to the side like weights.

I killed him.

Yes, for survival. But I killed Kingston.

I look up and watch as the spotlight continues to fly all around the arena bouncing off numerous blank faces in the crowd, all staring back at me in awe. No one believed I could survive.

If it wasn't for someone in the crowd to distract Kingston, our roles would had been reversed, leaving me the one laying lifeless on the arena floor and Kingston standing over me.

I achingly trudge the last few steps and shuffle my feet up to the edge of the transparent barrier. Slouched over in pain, I gaze into the crowd. *Now what?*

The spotlight continues to fly all around before landing on a small, secluded group of people close to the top. Inside the private box, a mysterious man in a dark suit stares back at me with piercing eyes and a grin, as if he has taken something of mine and knows it. He's older, with short dark hair, combed over, and a matching dark mustache. The man turns his head toward the person sitting next to him, cuing the spotlight to illuminate his petite guest.

It's a girl. She is sitting still and wearing a protective helmet over her face. The man fiddles with something behind her head, then removes the mask. The spotlight holds on the couple at the top. I already know who the girl is before the headgear is completely removed—Ria.

She wears a bewildered, muddled look across her face. Not worried or scared, but confused or perhaps sedated.

I pound a fist onto the wall in front of me and grit my teeth. *Who are these people?*

I sense one of the doors behind me slide open. I turn as three Tele soldiers enter the arena, all dressed in the same attire—black. Two of them have guns pointed at me, while the third uses his telekinetic force to transport Kingston off the floor and out the door. A small puddle of blood is the only thing left in his place.

I stare down at the pool of maroon. It's so dark it's almost purple. A folded-up, torn piece of paper halfway floats in the center of it, stained in red. I stretch and reach out for the paper, while at the same time eyeing the three Teles leaving the arena with Kingston's body.

Once they're gone, I unfold the red-stained paper, revealing only a single word written in a sloppy handwriting:

Virus

I glance back up at the man in the dark suit holding Ria, who is unaware of the note I just discovered. He smiles confidently back at me and places his hand on her shoulder.

I bang my fist up against the wall and open my mouth just as I feel a light pin prick to the back of my neck, zapping all of the energy out of me. I turn and collapse to the ground as I catch a glimpse of a man in a white lab coat holding a large needle standing over me.

He wears no expression, just a look of patience, waiting for me to—

And again…darkness.

CHAPTER 15

THE WASH

I blink my eyes open and force myself to wake up. I'm not sure how long I was out this time, but that same chalky taste is back in my mouth, this time accompanied by a piercing headache shooting through the middle of my forehead.

My eyes are fixed on the white tiled floor a few feet below me, telling me that I'm lying on my stomach. My head is positioned through a pre-cut hole in the bed large enough for my face to protrude, allowing me to breathe. I try pushing myself up, but I instantly feel the restraints. I'm strapped down to the bed. I can't move. A pair of tiny black dress shoes, much too small for a grown man to wear, shuffles over into my narrow field of vision.

"He should be waking up soon, Doctor Ledbetter," a young man's soft voice announces over me.

I try to speak, but there's a mouthguard lodged in my mouth, similar to the one on the plane.

"When he wakes," an older, deep voice begins, "give him a sedative and send him to the dorms. The Wash is now complete."

CHAPTER 16

ROOMMATE

"'Bout time you woke up," an annoyed, unknown voice calls down to me. "You've been snoring since they brought you in."

My eyes peek open and focus on the cot above me. The mattress sags down a few inches in the center telling me the voice came from the top bunk. I roll my head outward into my new room and it screams back at me in a bright white. Not only are the walls an alarming ghostly white, but so are the lights shining down from overhead, the sheets that cover me, the floor, even the sink and toilet that I can see through the open door across the room. Everything is coated with white, loud enough to give me an instant headache.

"I'm Logan by the way," the boy calls down to me again, this time in a more pleasant tone.

"Nic." My voice cracks as I say my name, so I clear my throat. "How long have I been out?"

"Since they brought you in last night." He rolls over on his side and sticks his head down at me.

I let out a huge yawn and nod up in his direction. Logan has a thin face, almost egg-shaped, with dirty blond hair sticking a few inches up, cut like a Mohawk. He's older than me, maybe sixteen or seventeen years old.

"What is this place?"

Logan positions himself better and stares down at me from the top bunk. "The other day I overheard a soldier call this place the Compound." He leans down a few more inches before continuing.

"It seems to be some kind of Government-run Tele boot camp."

I swallow the information, my eyes lolling to the floor before finding Logan again. "How long have you been here?" I have so many questions, but how do I know I can even trust him? I naively put all my faith into Kingston and that almost got me killed.

"Not really sure," he answers. "A little longer than you. They really don't tell you much here about your past."

Without warning, the heavy steel door in front of our beds clicks before rising up into the ceiling.

"Come on," Logan says. He slides his legs over the side and jumps down from the top bunk. There's no ladder, so I'm assuming he does this all the time. "Let's change and get some breakfast."

I peel back my sheets to reveal a clean white T-shirt and matching sweatpants underneath. I watch Logan walk across the room and open a closet, just like in the last room I was in, with about a dozen long sleeve white shirts and pants—all hanging down from white plastic hangers. Two pairs of white sneakers and black boots are lined up next to each other, below the clothes, as if that is how we left them before going to bed last night.

As I push myself up off the bottom cot, my body reminds me of how sore I am. My left arm is difficult to lift up more than a few inches and a large kink in my neck is preventing me from turning my head all the way to the side. I walk over to the lone mirror in the room to survey the damage. "What's with all the white anyway?"

"No clue." Logan slides off his T-shirt. He replaces it with an identical-looking one before tossing me a new shirt and a pair of pants. "Everyone wears it here but the soldiers."

I turn away and glance at myself in the mirror. No bruises or cuts on my face. That's strange. It appears the battle with Kingston took place months ago, giving me time to heal, but my aching body cries out something different.

Without any more discussion, we change into matching clothes (me changing in private in the bathroom with the door closed) and exit the small room. We fall in line with another group of teenage Teles also making their way down the same hallway. The walls are painted the same intense color of white as the room, with open doors on either side of us every few feet. Made bunk beds stare back at us, as I follow Logan and the group down the winding hallway. Large signs are posted between every other room on both sides of the corridor with slogans like:

—

It's Your Choice
Make a Difference
and
It's Your Duty to Serve

—

Once our tunnel begins to open up, I can hear voices chattering about all sorts of different things. We step through the open doors of the mess hall, and I take a look around. Long metallic tables and benches run up and down the room, all glistening back at me. They give the appearance of cleanliness or pureness. In order to continue its theme, the dining room's walls are painted the same awful white color matching everyone's clothes around me. Tele soldiers line the walls in their black uniforms, standing at attention, each holding a strapped gun in their hands.

Logan halts a dozen or so steps in front of me and turns, just now noticing that I'm still standing back in the doorway. "You coming?"

My eyes widen, nodding, taking in my new surroundings.

He shows me where the food trays are kept, and we both grab one, along with a single plate, a plastic spork, and a milk carton. We make our way through the food line before finding two empty seats in the back of the cafeteria by the exit.

"Brit and Tucker." Logan nods at two recruits already seated at the table we approach before joining them. "We're all from Ares."

Brit has short, rumpled red hair with freckles scattered across his nose and cheeks. His white T-shirt is at least a couple sizes too small for him, making him appear to be more overweight than he really is. Two dark circles line the bottom of his eyes. Tucker is the complete opposite. He has curly brown hair, pulled back behind his head. He's tall, tan, and appears to be athletic. Both recruits seem to be around the age of Logan.

I place my tray down and nod at both of them. They look up, but neither speaks as they continue to shovel food into their mouths.

"This is Nic," Logan introduces me. "He's a newb. Got here last night."

Tucker nods with a half smile, greeting me, while Brit's ghostly, gray eyes stare forward, his thoughts somewhere else entirely.

I dig my spork into what this place calls food and hold up a runny clump of white mush in front of my face before dropping it back onto the pile in the center of my plate. Along with the mush, two skinny strips of brown meat covered in gristle and fat and a single piece of cold toast stare back at me from my plate. I drop the plastic utensil and reach for the toast, it being the only thing I recognize. I watch Logan sit across from me, an arm on either side of his tray as if on guard, staring down at his breakfast. He wolfs the food down as fast as he can, as if it's the best thing he has ever tasted.

"Do they take it away if we don't eat fast enough?" I jab at him, forcing down a large bite of the dry toast. My stomach rumbles, reminding me that I haven't had a good meal in days, possibly weeks.

Logan looks up, piqued, just after he shovels in a large spoonful of the white mush. "It's all you're gonna get until lunch," he says with his mouth full, "so you may wanna eat."

He looks down at my plate and eyes my food, before glancing back up at me. His eyes widen, clearly looking behind me.

"You think you're special?" A high, shrill voice sounds, followed by a dark shadow looming over me.

I turn as the boy behind me dumps his entire milk carton over my head, confident he will not get caught. The milk cascades down my face and neck and forms a shallow puddle in my lap and on the floor all around me.

I start to get up, but feel a hand forcefully push me back down into my seat. On either side of the boy who's still holding out the milk carton in his hand, stands two big teen boys, both slouched over. The one on the left tightens his grip around my shoulder blade.

"Don't even think about getting up," the boy in the middle commands with authority. He wears the same white uniform as the rest of us, bearing the name Randall across his left shirt pocket. He has short dark hair, combed forward. His eyes scream hatred, as if he recognizes me and I talked bad about his mom or something. "Finish your breakfast. It could be your last."

The boy standing to the right takes his cue and scoops up a big helping of the white slop off my plate and plops it down on the center of my head. He mixes it in my already milk-soaked hair with the spork.

"We'll be paying you a visit later on, Nicholas. You can count on that." Randall laughs to himself before turning and walking away, his two goons on his heels.

"What was that?" I expel, finally finding my voice. I wipe a big glob of white mush from my hair and fling it back on my plate.

"That was Chaz Randall. Been here longer than any of us." Logan takes a bite from his toast before moving it around his plate, soaking up the remains of his breakfast. "He may not be big, but the dude's nuts."

"Yeah, I once heard he decapitated some kid in the arena— literally popped his noggin right off the kid's body," Brit says, joining in the conversation. His eyes widen before taking a quick look around. His story ends as fast as it started, as if someone signaled him to shut up. He picks up the last remaining strip of meat off his plate and tears a big bite off it.

Logan looks over at Brit and shakes his head. "Either way, just stay out of Chaz's way. Trust me on this one."

CHAPTER 17

TINY BLACK DRESS SHOES

After a quick shower and another change of clothes, I'm off to meet Logan for combat training. The hallway is just as congested as it was earlier, with the majority of the people heading in the same direction to the dojo.

Most of the conversations surrounding me are not what I expected. Instead of kids discussing how they can escape this place, most are conversing about whatever morning activity they are heading off to or about the food served at breakfast.

I crane my neck around a tall boy in front of me and notice a pair of adults walking against the flow of traffic, coming toward us. The two middle-aged men weave their way through the crowd, careful not to make contact with anyone. Both men wear their short hair neatly parted to the side, along with matching white lab coats buttoned all the way up to their collars. The tip of a bright red tie sneaks out of the top of each of the men's coats.

Other than being the only adults here, something about them seems out of place. As they approach, I study their faces. They seem pretty ordinary. No facial hair or scars; even their expressions seem subdued.

One of the men bumps shoulders with the recruit next to me. He turns his head back in my direction. His searching eyes quickly find mine, forcing him to snap his head back around, red-faced, as if he was just caught in a lie.

I look down at the suspicious man's feet as the two men continue off in the opposite direction—tiny black dress shoes. Sure, black dress shoes are common, maybe even small ones, but that look was something else.

The man with the tiny dress shoes leans his head in toward his partner and says something low under his breath. Both men halt and turn back around, their eyes scanning the hallway.

Instinctively, I duck down and camouflage myself in a large moving group of recruits in front of me.

I watch as the men give up their search within seconds. The man with the tiny dress shoes pulls a key card off his belt to open a door labeled KEEP OUT, allowing his partner inside first. He takes one more quick scan of the hallway before entering the room, allowing the door to close behind him on its own.

I catch the door just before it shuts. I hold onto the edge of the cold steel frame, wide enough for only my fingers to squeeze through. Inside appears to be some kind of laboratory with countertops full of vials and test tubes with an assortment of multicolored liquids, along with microscopes and other mechanical devices and monitors that I've never seen before.

"Commander Lee is on the Prompter for you, Doctor Ledbetter," I hear a stern voice say, only to confirm my suspicions. "He wants to know how the Wash went with the new recruit, McCready, and if we have deciphered the note we found on him."

I watch as Doctor Ledbetter calmly walks over to where the other men are standing in the corner of the lab and holds up a glass tablet.

"Commander Lee, sir, the Wash was a success. As for the note we found"—the doctor adjusts his glasses and moves them up the bridge of his nose—"we'll have some answers before nightfall. I can promise you that. We have our ways."

I release a gasp; my hand knocks against the heavy door in front of me with a loud clack.

Both men turn as I release my grip on the door. I dive back into the steady torrent of Teles making their way to the dojo and pray the doctors didn't see me. Instead of trying to wrap my brain around what a Wash is, only one thought absorbs my head—how I'm going to escape out of this place before nightfall.

*   *   *

The winding hallway leads me and the rest of the recruits to the dojo. I enter through a set of opened double doors marked with a sign over them in big block letters that reads:

_____

UNLEASH YOUR GIFT

_____

I scan the room. It's at least twice as large as the arena, but with no bleachers or a transparent wall enclosing it. Mirrors line the walls, minus one section that is reflecting all black. A giant picture of a blackbird with a single red-starred eye covers the majority of the floor, painted over a thin layer of red matting under my feet. Tele soldiers, armed with automatic guns, stand at attention in various locations around the large hall.

I look for a familiar face as I walk around the individual mats scattered across the floor. The intense smell of a decade of sweat grows stronger the farther I move into the large room. No sign of Ria, Ren, or even the psycho August. Ria is the only one of the three I know for sure who was caught, but considering I haven't seen another girl here since I've arrived, I'm assuming they are holding her in a different location.

I spot Logan sitting all alone on a single mat, located on the far side of the dojo. A small white X is marked on the ground right across from where he is sitting. He points to it and motions for me to sit.

"I've gotta get out of here," I say in a low voice, sitting down and crossing my legs. I restlessly glance around the room and eye a large gun strapped around the neck of one of the many Tele soldiers on guard. Sweat trails down the middle of my back.

"Because of what Chaz Randall said?" He looks up, as if he's thinking of an answer to his own question. "Impossible," he says in a low voice. He covers his mouth with the side of his hand. "There are eyes everywhere."

I look up and follow his stare. Little white cameras spread out high across the dojo's ceiling. And with the mirrors lining the walls, it gives the cameras even more angles to watch over everyone.

"No one's ever escaped before."

"So it can't be done?" I fire back, as the lights begin to dim around us on their own.

Logan opens his mouth to answer, but is cutoff.

"I know a way out," a small voice jumps in from the mat in front of us. The boy turns his head back, but refuses to turn all the way around. He has short dark hair and skin to match, sitting with his knees pulled up toward his chest. He looks younger, maybe twelve or thirteen. He covers his mouth with his hand, careful not to get caught talking on camera.

We both nod at the boy. Logan studies the back of his head like he's not sure if he believes him or not.

"If you want out, I've heard the only place is through the hangar."

"The drone hangar?" Logan questions, twisting up his face. His eyes process the information. "Makes sense." He raises and drops a single shoulder blade, before nodding his head in approval. "It's the only place I know of that has access to the ground level other than the elevators."

"Ground level?"

Both Logan and the recruit let out a small chuckle at the same time.

"He's new." Logan informs the boy in front of us.

"Oh yeah, your buddy Nic there is famous," the recruit says a little louder, still covering his mouth when he speaks. "Everyone's been talking about him since he took down the mighty Kingston in the arena last night."

A series of loud beeps sounds over the loudspeaker. Everyone's attention moves to the dark monitor at the front of the room. The screen takes up the entire front wall, easily large enough for everyone to see it.

"Today you will learn about the pressure points of the human body," a calm, mechanical-sounding voice begins over the loudspeaker, filling the hushed room. "You cannot rely only on your gift in combat situations; you must learn to use other abilities when fighting your enemy."

An image of a human body pops up on the monitor, diagramming all the pressure point locations and how sensitive each area is. A video begins showing different combat moves and how to attack your enemies' pressure points with ease.

"You're never gonna make it," Logan mumbles under his breath, eyes still glued to the monitor in front of him as if he didn't say it.

A Tele soldier trudges up from behind and stops to Logan's left in his blind spot. The expression on Logan's face tells me he's aware we have company.

"Say something, recruit?" The Tele soldier is covered in the standard black uniform. He wears a Tele shell over his clothes and a helmet covering the majority of his face. He flips open the lid on his headgear with one hand and stares down at Logan. He grips his gun with his other hand, his index finger already in place behind the trigger.

"No, sir," Logan spits out. He gives the soldier what he wanted to hear, forcing him to move on to torment another recruit farther up in line.

"You don't understand," I whisper back. I take my eyes off the screen for a few seconds, spying on Logan. The note I discovered lying partially hidden in Kingston's pool of blood, pops back in my head—*Virus*. Just the single word. No hints. No direction—just *Virus*. "I just have to get outta here," I repeat. "Tonight."

CHAPTER 18

ALL ACCESS

Following combat training and then lunch—and then even more training—the people in charge finally award us with some much-needed downtime. Most recruits hangout in their rooms going over what they learned earlier in the day, while others roam the halls trying to pass time before lights out.

I don't plan to be here at lights out.

I can't be.

"Your one chance of making it to the hangar is through the catwalk." Logan sits backwards in a chair a few feet away from the cot, elbows up on the back's ledge. He motions down the hall with a nod of his head. "But you'll need a key card just to get in. All the doors here are like that."

I scratch at the back of my neck, assumingly where a scarred up blackbird tattoo is now in place after the Wash was performed. The doctor's warning from earlier still echoes throughout my head.

"And then you have the cameras to watch out for." Logan lowers his voice as a large pack of recruits noisily walk by our room discussing the training from earlier in the day. "They're everywhere."

"Well, well, well. Looky who it is," a familiar high, shrill voice cuts in from the doorway. Chaz Randall glances down the hallway, checking to see if anyone is watching before stepping into our room uninvited with his two thugs, again, on either side of him. This time I have an opportunity to read the names on their shirts: Curtis and

Faber.

"Chaz," Logan acknowledges our unwelcome guest, exhaling his name.

I tense up and straighten the arch in my back. Chaz takes a couple more steps forward, ignoring Logan. He eyes me the whole time.

"Everyone's up in arms talking about you ever since your little battle with Kingston the other night, but I think you just got lucky is all." Chaz spits on the floor. His permanent scowl stays on his face. Curtis and Faber remain silent, arms crossed.

I find the glob of spit on the floor between us, just as my stomach releases a loud grumble. I really wish I'd eaten more today. I force my eyes back up to Chaz.

"A fatty like you could never defeat a true soldier like me in the arena." Chaz pats the center of his chest. "I'm surprised you can even lift your fat self off the cot there," he says, amusing himself. He nudges Faber standing to his right, cuing him to laugh. "Let alone how it even holds you."

I bite down hard on my bottom lip and exhale through my nose so the whole room can hear.

"Hey, I'm talking to you, Pig—" He begins to mouth the name I despise more than anything else.

The nickname rings throughout my head, even before Chaz can finish saying it.

I flick my hand up, and in a flash send Chaz shooting backward. His body flies across the hall, slamming into the brick wall of the neighboring room. The back of his head thumps loudly, before his body falls to the ground. Chaz's two minions rush to his side to check on him.

"You shouldn't have done that, Nic." Logan's face goes ashen. His stare shoots back and forth between me and Chaz, who is still lying unconscious on the floor across the hall. "It's against the rules to use your powers here unless you're battling in the arena or the dojo. Plus," he adds, "the dude's wacked in the head."

I jump up off my bed, only to meet an armed Tele soldier in the doorway. He glances at me and grips his gun, before deciding to turn to check on Chaz. A small, growing crowd has gathered between the two rooms, congesting the hallway. A second Tele soldier arrives and has to fight his way through the crowd before entering our room. Logan jumps up from his seat, back pressed up against the wall, standing behind the second soldier.

My hands shoot up in the air, as I take a step back toward my cot. The second soldier wears the standard Tele shell over his black uniform to block any telekinetic attack I might try.

"You responsible for this, recruit?" the Tele soldier's mechanical voice asks through his closed helmet. He's just confirming what he already knows.

Before I can respond, Faber flies through the doorway and barrels into me. His sudden brute force knocks me back onto my cot, stunning me. In the process, one of his long flailing arms smacks the Tele soldier across the back of the head and knocks him off balance. The soldier's heavy gun clunks to the ground and skids across the floor.

Back on my bed, I raise my arms in an attempt to block the barrage of blows being unleashed from Faber sitting on top of me. He pins my hands down with his one free arm across my body, as he tries to choke the life out of me with his other. He grunts as he drives my head back at a ninety-degree angle.

Logan doesn't hesitate to pick up the gun. He rushes over to the large mammoth holding me down and raises the weapon high above his head, before bringing the butt of it down across the back of Faber's skull. The boy rolls off me with a surprised moan and falls to the side.

I push myself gingerly off the bed, dazed.

"Here!" Logan places something thin and rectangular in my palm before closing my fingers around it. "Get down the hall and stay to your right. Find the catwalk!"

Without question, I nod before propelling myself out of our room and through the crowd. It seems like everyone in the Compound has gathered outside in the hallway.

"Halt!" I hear voices bark out from behind. I turn my head to glance back and run into a large group of Tele soldiers, all armed, rushing off in the direction of the chaos.

The unexpected contact drops me to the ground in front of one soldier. I look up, only to meet the barrel of his gun inches away from my forehead. The Tele soldier grips the handle and scowls down at me, helmet visor already raised.

"Where are you off to in such a hurry, recruit?" He squints his eyes while looking down at me. He appears much larger than he really is.

I open my mouth, knowing full well I'm done for.

"I...ah..." I look away. "I was..."

The Tele soldier holds out a hand and silences me, before pressing a button on the side of his helmet to turn on his earpiece. He pauses long enough to process the information received before lowering his gun. He flips the helmet's visor back down with his free hand and takes off again without saying another word.

I shake my head, push myself up, and get back on my feet. I want to create as much space between myself and this chaotic place as I can.

A steady flow of recruits continues to dash by me, all heading in the opposite direction. I look up and pass a security camera recording my escape. They'll be on me before I know it. I keep going, though. I keep staying to my right, just like Logan said, until I finally come to a door labeled: CATWALK. KEEP OUT.

I reach out for the handle. It's locked. A small electronic keypad is lit up to the right of the door. For the first time since entering the hallway I look down and open up my hand. A little white key card that reads ALL ACCESS across the front of it in big, bold letters stares back at me. I swipe the key reader using the card, releasing a click and unlocking the door. I step inside, into the darkness, shutting the door and the madness out behind me.

I have no idea why or how he did it, but thank you, Logan. Thank you.

CHAPTER 19

INSIDE AN ELEVATOR

It's cold and dark inside the catwalk. I stand frozen with the door to my back, too timid to take a step forward. A cold, musty smell enters my nostrils, not giving me the slightest hint about my clandestine surroundings. I reach out in front of me and bang my hand hard up against something solid about a half an inch thick, running horizontally across my face in the shape of a narrow pipe. I reach up finding another bar about a foot up. An image of a ladder mounted to the wall in front of me pops in my head. I pull down on the first rung to make sure it holds.

Seems strong enough.

I take my small first step out, the toes in my shoe suddenly not finding solid ground underneath. The ladder must go both ways—up and down. I reach back out and grip onto the first two metal bars. I wonder how far down it goes. A hundred feet? A thousand? I have no clue. Afraid of the inevitable, I peer down into the invisible hole that I know surrounds the ladder. Only the sound of cool air comes back out. I shake my head. With everything I've been through, this is nothing.

I reach out with both hands and begin my climb.

I pull myself up, one bar at a time, until a sudden nearby noise forces me to halt. The ladder wobbles, suspending me in the dark.

Voices.

Securing myself, I grip onto the ladder and wrap both arms around the rung positioned in front of me, trying to listen. I know who the voices are looking for—me. By now, the Tele soldier who Logan swiped the key card from has to have figured out it is missing. The small, rectangular plastic card rubs up against my inner thigh, reaffirming it's still in my pocket.

Muffled voices yell something out through the walls behind me, not clear enough for me to make out.

I tell myself to keep going.

I continue the steady climb up before my forearms and aching shoulders begin to tense up. A cramp shoots through one of my legs. I halt.

Voices again.

This time from below.

I peer down as a door creaks opens. The tiny crawlspace lights up.

"Hey! There he is!" A voice echoes out. It sounds much closer than the light makes it appear.

"Freeze!"

Multiple guns enter my view, along with the blurred faces of three Tele soldiers staring up at me.

"Fire the Tocsin!"

Seconds later, a loud shot goes off from below.

Boom!

An immediate silver light explodes all around me. It lights up the narrow crawlspace bright enough to convince me that someone just turned on the spotlight of a lighthouse, forcing me to close my eyes.

I shudder because I know what comes next.

An ear-piercing alarm sounds in my ears. It cuts through my head like a knife. I'm forced to release my grip on the ladder, my hands over my ears. I drop, luckily landing only a few feet down on my side and roll onto a nearby platform. I reach up and pull down on the handle to the door in front of me, sliding myself out into the hallway, exiting the catwalk. My whole body aches reminding me of the arena.

I arduously scoot myself backward and press my back up against the closed door, finally able to open my eyes.

I inspect my new surroundings while taking in several deep breaths of air.

The new floor I'm on looks identical to the last one, but with one notable difference: it's covered in black. I look in the corner above the door I exited and discover a small black camera staring back at me out of reach. A little red light blinks in my direction informing the people in charge of my exact location. I lift up my hand and pull the camera clean off the wall. It falls to the ground next to me, multicolor wires hanging out the back of it. I levitate it and fling it across the room, smashing it in a hundred pieces against a nearby wall.

They'll be here any second.

More voices.

I hear them before they come in view. A small group of three recruits dressed in black approach me from down the hall. I watch as they step around the broken video camera lying in the middle of the floor.

I lift myself up from off the floor, using an almost full laundry cart positioned in the corner of the hallway as leverage. I reach in and grab a black T-shirt and matching pants off the top of the pile.

I look around and spot a small nearby closet located next to the elevators. I produce my key card and unlock the door. The overpowering smell of chemicals hits me as I open the door before ducking inside. I'm in some kind of cleaning supplies closet. I change out of my whites, replacing them with the black. The shirt is a little tight on me and the pant legs only come down to just above my ankles, but they'll have to do. I stuff my whites behind a few bottles of bleach down on the floor before cracking open the door.

The hallway is empty.

Now what?

I turn and find a set of closed elevator doors. A motivational poster is on display on the wall next to them, reading:

———

See Yourself as the Way You WILL Be, Not the Way You USED to Be

———

I reach into my pocket and produce the key card again, swiping the elevator doors. Seconds later, I hear a single beep, but only to be followed by the catwalk's door flying open behind me.

The elevator rings out another single beep. The doors open. Stepping forward, I glance back. The tip of a gun barrel inches into view, protruding out of the open doorway, followed by multiple Tele soldiers dressed in black.

"Halt!" The first soldier rushes over to the elevator. "You're in violation of Code 11-76. Freeze or we'll be forced to shoot!"

The elevator doors begin to come together, sealing me in, as a familiar face flashes before me, our eyes meeting—

Rollins!

CHAPTER 20

OF THE EARTH

As the elevator moves up floors, I sink to the ground. My mind's racing. Rollins is *here?* And he's working for the same people who took him? Images from a year ago enter my head—the night my brother was taken by the Government for being a Tele; a crime where we come from, rather where we *came* from. I shake my head trying to wrap my brain around all of this, but it doesn't add up.

The elevator comes to a screeching halt. A single beep rings out through the speaker above me. The doors slide open. Top floor.

I peek my head out and wait for an ambush. But it doesn't come. Strangely enough, the place seems to be empty. The walls are painted jet black with minimal light overhead. Only every third light is turned on, ready to guide me down the hallway.

I step out of the elevator, again listening for voices, sounds, something. My shoes squeak, echoing off the glossy black floor, breaking the silence. I hear a loud grinding noise, almost like metal on metal up ahead, followed by something that sounds like a fire extinguisher being sprayed.

A light flashes on over me, followed by another, and then again another. Each one mirrors my squeaky footsteps down the hall. The overhead lights must be motion-detected.

The short hallway ends and opens into a much larger room, bigger than both the dojo and arena combined. Huge florescent lights flick on over me illuminating the entire laboratory. Long metallic countertops line the walls with an open, spacious center filled with dozens of aerial drones, both ShadowHawks and ShadowEagles combined. The main difference between the two is the size. Hawks are slightly smaller, unmanned drones, while Eagles can fit up to three passengers.

I've never been this close to an inactive drone before.

I run my hand down the body of one of the Eagles, gently touching it with just my fingertips, measuring the length of the aircraft. Above each drone, a large circular steel plate sits in the ceiling, the same length and width as the aircraft. An image of a large blackbird is embedded into the steel plate facing down, as if it's watching over the Eagle. The same logo is displayed on either side of the drone—a blackbird with a red star for its eye. A bulky, thick rubber tube connects from the side of the drone to the plate in the ceiling. Possibly its power source?

I realize now the loud noise I heard down the hallway was a Hawk returning to the hangar. The ceiling is still in the process of sealing itself over the drone, sliding back into place. I walk up to the newly arrived unmanned aircraft and place my hand on the side of its body.

It's still warm.

I look up and examine the ceiling overhead completing its shift closed. It looks like a giant steel plate slowly being positioned to fit over the hole. Once it's sealed, a loud horn buzzes and a single red light hanging over the flying device flips on. A green bulb remains turned off, located next to the flashing red light.

The ceiling is now sealed over.

Silence.

I look around the lab. A computer tablet is turned on, glowing from across the room. I rush over to it and study the device. A lengthy list of three-digit numbers runs down the left side of the screen, each containing the same pair of lights—red and green. Almost a dozen of them are glowing green. Possibly Hawks or Eagles out on missions?

I slide my fingers down the screen to the bottom of the page. Near the end of the list, I spot one drone blinking back at me with a stopwatch enumerating down—thirty seconds and counting.

A loud click echoes out from the ceiling and I duck behind one of the countertops. The roof begins to slide over so I get a view of the outside world for the first time since the plane crashed in the woods.

The sun has already started to set, producing a long, dark shadow that creeps across the hangar floor.

I drop the tablet on the countertop and rush over to the launch pad.

A ShadowHawk lowers itself through the opening in the ceiling and fills a once-open spot on the floor. A blue flame breathes out of the back of the drone for another ten seconds or so before extinguishing on its own. The Hawk then releases a mechanical groan, followed by a number of clicks. It relaxes itself a few more feet closer to the ground. A large rubber tube falls from the ceiling and connects itself to the body of the drone.

I guess this place runs on its own.

I extend out my hand and place my fingertips on the surface of the unmanned aircraft. It's still warm from the sun, but bearable.

I reach up with both arms and lift myself up onto the Hawk's wing. The drone surprisingly doesn't teeter. It holds a firm position. My eyes move up to the closing hole above me…the short distance to freedom just out of reach. Already more than halfway through its landing procedure, I know any minute now the ceiling will seal shut.

I grab a hold of the thick black rubber tube running down the side of the Hawk, connected to the ceiling, and begin to climb. I shimmy myself up the cylindrical device, the rubber tubing swaying back and forth with each movement making it even more difficult to climb.

Voices.

Shouting.

I freeze, vulnerably hanging midway up the tube. The muscles in my forearms begin to ache, begging to be released. I look back over my shoulder across the laboratory floor.

"McCready, freeze!" a voice shouts out from across the lab, followed by a group of armed Tele soldiers rushing toward me. The soldier in the lead has his gun aimed at me, as do the four other soldiers behind him shuffling across the shiny floor. All five soldiers are wearing protective headgear and shells. Is Rollins one of them?

I lift my head up and calculate the distance to the top. The steel plate continues to grind its way across the opening, closing off the light from outside.

It's now or never. I don't have time to wait for another drone to arrive.

I jump and release my hold from the rubber tube, reaching for the sky. Both of my hands find the outer edge, but there's nothing to grip onto. I feel the tips of my fingers slipping backward, bringing me back down through the hole.

"Freeze or we'll be forced to shoot!"

I dig my fingernails into the dirt on the other side, my weight pulling me back down. My feet kick at air, striking the side of the solid rubber tubing over and over. I feel someone grab and pull at my ankle.

My left hand loses its grip from above and a clump of dirt falls into my eyes. I flip my palm up through the opening, aiming it at whatever's nearby.

I sense something close, secured to the ground—maybe a building or something too heavy to move? The force yanks me right out of the hole, as if in a wind tunnel, and I release my grip on the unknown object in midair. I tumble to the ground, the hard earth scraping at my knees; I'm exhausted and out of breath.

The steel plate continues to slide itself shut the final few feet beside me and seals the outside world off from the Compound. I hear a loud horn sound below me, signaling the drone return is complete. I roll myself to the side, all of the muscles in my body screaming out in pain. I made it, but I know this is just the start.

CHAPTER 21

ONLY ONE

Even though the sun is setting, I immediately feel its warmth on my skin. I lay on my back, my chest heaving up and down fighting to catch my breath. The faint smell of salt enters my nostrils. I lift myself halfway up off the ground, hug my knees, and look around. I expected some kind of ambush—a group of Tele soldiers huddled together with their guns already on me—but again, I'm alone.

An uprooted tree nearby clues me in on what assisted me out of the hole. The tree still sways back and forth with not a hint of wind around. I scoot back against the trunk to rest for a second. My original plan ended with an escape from the Compound, but now what?

A familiar loud metal on metal sound resonates behind me, shaking the ground I'm sitting on. My head flies around to watch another launching pad open. I hear a siren going off down below as the steel plate inches its way over.

I have to move.

I have no clue where I'm going, but my first order of business is to put as much distance as possible between myself and the Compound. The images of my brother, Ria, Ren, Logan and even August all enter my head. *My friends.* The idea of having a friend, let alone multiple people who I could count on was foreign to me in my pervious life, and now I'm just going to leave them all behind?

I break off into a run, slicing down a narrow path cut with trees until my body feels like it's about to give out. I collapse my weight onto the side of an old magnolia tree, the only thing keeping me on my feet. The back of my throat stings as if I'm having to fight my lungs for fresh oxygen. What I would do for some water right now.

I lift up my head to look back in the direction of the Compound. The forest has swallowed the launching pads area whole, not giving me the slightest hint of how far I've run. My body tells me otherwise. Ignoring the pain, I force myself off the large tree and back into a sprint.

The sun is now almost set, darkness creeping in. I hear a loud noise up ahead, the sound of water crashing back and forth.

And then I see it.

How is this even possible?

Just ahead of me, as the land begins to slope down, maybe twenty yards away is the ocean. Am I back in Sol? Maybe I never left? But a plane took us up in the air…

Bam!

Zap!

I strike something head on, spewing me backward. My unconscious body flies a few feet through the air, before collapsing to the ground.

*　　*　　*

"He's beginning to wake, Doctor Ledbetter."

"Good. Get Commander Lee up on the Prompter. Let him know the recruit has awakened."

Multiple voices flow over me. A pair of footsteps echoes across the tile floor, as they move away. My head still feels groggy, with all of my limbs numb. A mouthguard has been lodged between my teeth again, silencing me. I attempt to turn my head, but realize it's impossible. I'm paralyzed.

Possibly some kind of numbing agent?

Unlike after the Wash, this time I have been placed on my back. A man in a white lab coat wheels my gurney around before unhooking a couple of latches underneath the hospital bed, raising my entire body up. The sudden shift makes it appear as if I'm standing up against a thin wall of mattresses.

I shoot my gaze around the room. The same awful bright white paint flashes back, telling me I'm back on my original floor in the Compound. The same metallic countertops line the walls, with various computers and other scientific items placed around the lab.

"You're lucky, kid. Normally, Commander Lee would just send you to Re-Ed with the rest of the traitors." Doctor Ledbetter snorts and looks off to the side. "But for some reason, he's decided to meet with you first. Now behave yourself." His tone scolds me like a father figure, warning me to play nice.

I glance down at his shoes, my eyes and ears being the only thing I have any control over. Seeing his tiny, women-like feet again almost causes a smile to creep up on my face.

The doctor sticks his gloved hand into my mouth and removes the mouthpiece.

Another man in a white lab coat walks over from across the room and places a large tablet before me. The screen is blank, but only for a few seconds.

A man's face, mostly hidden in dark shadows, appears on the tablet, looking down. He has short dark brown hair, combed over to the side in a part. He wears a dark suit with a white, open-collared, button-up shirt underneath, the first three buttons unhooked. The look on his face makes him appear calm, but as soon as he glances up, our eyes meet, and his expression changes. A stern look grows across his face like a dark shadow.

"Nicholas, it seems you have found our security fence." His thin eyebrows rise in a slant; a smile crosses his face.

I think back to the last thing I remember. *The ocean.* The image of waves crashing onto shore only a dozen or so yards in front of me comes rushing back. And then the jolt; so it was a fence I smacked into? Some kind of invisible barrier—like in the arena, but electrified?

Commander Lee pauses, as if he's waiting for me to respond before continuing, "But you should know by now there's no escape." He lightly scratches at the side of his head with the tip of his index finger. "Besides, where would you go? It's against the law to be a Tele in Sol." A menacing smile forms across the commander's face. He knows he has me. I have no place to run. "We're here to help you, Nicholas. We're here to show you how to use your gift to its full extent. Don't fight it."

I open my mouth, not quite sure what to say. I glance over at Doctor Ledbetter. He is focused on the Prompter's screen, along with the other two men in white lab coats standing on either side of me. Commander Lee is clearly running the show here, not the doctors.

"I'm surprised you haven't asked about your friends yet."

An image of Rollins pops in my head, followed by one of Ria.

"Where are you keeping her?" I break my silence. "Is she okay?"

The menacing smile doesn't leave the commander's face. If anything, it grows. "Ria Farris? Oh, she's fine. I'm glad you brought her up, actually." Commander Lee pauses again, his eyes trained on mine, studying me, before turning to the side and looking over his shoulder. A powerful, glowing light clicks on and illuminates his surroundings.

The camera focuses on a girl in a cell behind the commander.

The side of my neck twitches.

Before the camera can come into focus, I know who the girl is— Ria.

"As you can see, she's fine."

Ria paces back and forth in her cell, a room only big enough to hold a small cot and a toilet. She doesn't look up as if she's unaware she is even being filmed.

Maybe she's been drugged?

"Ria," I scream out, trying to get her attention. "It's me, Nic!" With my face still paralyzed, my expression doesn't change. "Ria!"

The girl on the other side of the Prompter doesn't even flinch at the sound of my voice. She continues to pace from one end of her cell to the other, completely in her own world.

"Save your breath, Nicholas. She can't hear you. The walls have been soundproofed and darkened." Commander Lee leans forward to clarify, his eyes glowing malignantly. "You can see her, but she can't see you."

I release a deep exhale through my nose, feeling helpless. I wait for the commander to continue.

"I've thought long and hard about this." The lights shut off behind him, a sheet of darkness falling over Ria's holding cell. "You must be punished for trying to escape the Compound. There's no question about it."

My eyes widen, waiting to hear what the commander will say next.

"You and your little friend, Ria, will battle against each other in the arena." Commander Lee leans forward, his face taking up the entire screen again. "And as always, there can only be one winner."

His lips begin to curl up, his eyebrows slanting, pointing down toward the tip of his nose. "Good luck, Nicholas."

The screen goes black.

Signal lost.

CHAPTER 22

BE READY

I stand forlorn in front of the door of my cell, made up of steel bars running all the way down to the floor. The numbing agent has worn off, but the thought of being forced to battle Ria has not yet settled in.

They can't make us fight...can they? The horrific night I was forced to battle Kingston comes rushing back at me. I answer my own question. It was obvious neither of us wanted to battle, but regardless, I ended up killing him in the arena. I try to push away the image of Kingston's lifeless face, surrounded by a pool of his own blood, but it sticks in the back of my mind like a bad reminder.

The image of Ria on the ground like that makes me shudder.

"Dinner!" I hear a Tele soldier call out from down the hall, sliding food trays into the small openings between the horizontal bars of each cell.

A tray slides halfway in on the ledge. Nothing looks edible but a single chocolate chip cookie placed on a folded napkin on the edge of the tray. I pick up the cookie and take a large bite out of it. Like everything else here, it's bland and over-cooked. I pop the rest of the cookie into my mouth before picking up the napkin, wiping away the crumbs from the corners of my mouth.

Words.

I look down at the folded up napkin and flip it over, studying it. Written in really tiny handwriting, down on the corner of the napkin are two words: Be ready.

I raise my eyebrows and tear off the corner of the napkin with the message scribbled on it. Without hesitation, I pop the corner of the napkin in my mouth, swallowing it. I open up the single serving milk carton and take a big gulp. Be ready for what exactly?

*   *   *

The lamp clicks on overhead just like every other morning, ordering me out of bed. I haven't slept well in days, my mind only on one thing—Ria.

"Time to get up, McCready. Today's your big day." A Tele soldier peers in through the bars. "Get dressed. I'll be back in five to take you to the arena."

I lift my legs out of bed and scratch at the back of my neck. The tattoo from the Wash still itches, a constant reminder they already have some control over me. From the sitting position, I raise up my palm and direct it toward the closet. The closet door opens on its own, followed by a white shirt and pants floating across the short distance to me. I change and leave my nightclothes on the bed.

Just as I'm tying my shoes, a loud click rings out, sending the door of bars rising up into the ceiling. Two Tele soldiers are there to escort me to the arena.

This time, I go without a fight. I glare up at a security camera on the way to the elevators, passing it, being led down the hall. I think back to when I tried to escape the first time—my first failed attempt—and how they were on me before I could even flee the floor.

The elevator rings out a beep, warning us the doors are about to open. As we step in, very clearly, I hear the words whispered from behind, "Be ready, Nic."

I turn my head in both directions. Neither guard flinches, hinting one uttered the words.

The bell rings out again; the doors close us in.

Did I just imagine that? Am I hearing voices in my head now?

Following another beep, the elevator doors open with the two Tele soldiers guiding me out. We march down another couple of sets of hallways to a closed red door at the bottom of a stairwell.

I already know what's on the other side.

The soldier in the lead halts just long enough to swipe his keycard on the reader. Muffled music blares through the steel door mixed in with the sounds of an impatient crowd waiting for the impending battle to begin.

After a loud click, the door rises up on its own. A spotlight is flying around the arena illuminating the faces in the crowd. I peer through the invisible wall separating us from the onlookers, again relieved it's there. A neon red haze begins to mushroom around the arena, Teles being activated before my very eyes.

The door across from me begins to rise; a narrow shadow eerily creeps across the arena floor. Ria takes a single step out, a new song to welcome her beginning over the speakers.

"Ladies and gentlemen, we have a treat for you tonight." The unknown announcer cuts through the music with his deep, booming voice. "A battle of the sexes if you will. In one corner, we have undefeated at one-to-nothing, Recruit Nicholas McCready!" The announcer pauses, allowing the crowd to cheer, mixed in with some minor heckling.

My eyes are fixed on Ria. I block everything else out. I study her face, her body language. She stands frozen, as if she waits to be commanded forward. Stiff. Her eyes burn holes through me.

"And in the other corner," the booming voice cuts back in, "we have undefeated at two-and-zero, Recruit Ria Farris!"

The first time Ria and I met on the plane comes back to me. I can still feel the effects of her powerful kick that left me sprawled out on the cockpit floor, dazed. I rub at the edge of my chin reminiscing about the strong blow to the head. Even if I *wanted* to battle her, I'm not so sure I could defeat her.

Ria's entrance music dies, but the majority of the crowd continues their own chant, beating their fists—both in the air and against the see-through barrier in front of them. They're ready for the battle.

I take a couple of small steps forward; Ria mirrors my move.

I spin my head around, my eyes cataloguing the arena floor. Various objects lay in the four corners of the room like in the previous battle with Kingston. *Wait, what am I doing? I can't use a weapon on Ria.* Somehow I have to figure out a way for both of us to escape unharmed.

I turn my attention back in front of me in time to see Ria flip her hand up. My body goes weightless, rocketing back and banging against the protective barrier behind me. My head hits first and bounces off the wall with a thud. I let out a low groan.

Ria charges at me, the hostile look on her face telling me she wants to rip my head off.

I stick my hand up just in time and lift Ria off the ground, spinning her around and around in the air. I know the move won't harm her; at the very most it might make her feel a little nauseous. Her little body whirls like a tornado a few feet off the ground, until... Bam!

A rogue wave of telekinetic force washes over me and knocks me back a few feet on my back.

Ria lands in front of me in a fighting stance...her kick is the reason why I'm on the ground. She punches in the air, her own unique form of Tele martial arts, and a barrage of waves strike me over and over from at least ten feet across the room. My head flies back, then to the side, followed by multiple punches to the gut. I slump over with a whimper, holding the middle of my stomach with both hands.

I feel dizzy.

I try to get up and fall back to the ground.

The punching has ceased. Is Ria feeling sorry for me?

I steal a quick glance up. My vision is blurred; my head feels like it's swimming. I try to focus on the shadow moving across the arena floor—Ria's—but it's shaky. She stands in the corner, her back to me, examining the weapons before her. The most damaging item I can make out is an old refrigerator missing its front handle.

Slowly, the fridge begins to levitate. Both of Ria's hands rise over her head, the old refrigerator mimicking her motions. She faces me, holding the heavy object over herself as if it's weightless. A concerned look flashes across her face; she cannot locate me in the dark shadows of the arena floor. A spotlight comes to her aide and it illuminates my surroundings.

"Finish him," she calls out in a deep, commanding, evil tone, almost as if she's trying to convince herself. Her arms move back a few inches behind her head, ready to release the weapon and flatten me like a bug.

The door right behind an unaware Ria slides opens, shooting out a dark shadow, followed by a single Tele soldier. The soldier lifts his gun and shoots Ria in the back, forcing her to release the heavy object. The fridge tumbles out of her hands and crashes to the ground only a few feet in front of her. Ria collapses to the side. The Tele soldier grabs her, motioning his gun at me.

"Ready, Nic?" he calls out.

I get up and rush toward the opening, stepping into the darkness. I have no clue what's waiting for me on the other side of the door.

CHAPTER 23

OVER IT

As soon as the three of us are through, the door slides down, closing us off from the arena. We're in a dimly lit staircase. The Tele soldier clicks on a small helmet light, after placing Ria down in the corner of the stairwell. The soldier then flips the visor of his helmet up, his eyes waiting for me to speak.

"Hey, little bro, we gotta move." Rollins stares back at me.

I open my mouth, but he waves me off. "Later. Come on."

My brother grabs hold of my sleeve and pulls me halfway up the stairs; his other hand remains around the trigger of his gun.

"Wait!" I cry out, halting. "We can't just leave her here."

Rollins looks down at Ria before glancing back at me. Without saying another word, he bends down to pick her up and throws her over his shoulder as if she's weightless. "Now, come on."

He stomps up the stairs, leading the way down the winding hallway that appears identical to one I was just marched down. We come to a set of elevators marked: SERVICE ELEVATORS. The doors open as soon as Rollins swipes his keycard.

"Why?" I question. "Why are you working for them?"

The elevator climbs floor after floor. I already know where we are headed.

"They told me you were all dead." Rollins pauses, eyes fixed on the wall behind me. "They told me there was a terrorist attack in Sol, hitting our neighborhood—killing you, Mom, and Dad. I had no choice. No other place to turn."

I shake my head as I try to wrap my brain around all of this.

"Then they gave me the decision: either stay here and join Operation Blackbird or return to Sol and face charges on being a Tele. What choice did I have? And then I saw you the other day and…"

The elevator comes to a screeching halt. The lights flicker for a second before clicking off.

"There's no camera in here"—Rollins takes a quick glance around—"so I figured we had a chance to reach the hangar, but I guess they tracked us."

Rollins lifts both hands and directs them at the closed elevator doors in front of him. Within seconds, the doors part revealing that we've stopped between floors. He picks up his gun again and straps it across his back. In the year Rollins has been gone he has bulked up considerably. Muscles now protrude out of his shirt, saying goodbye to the tall, slender brother I grew up with.

Rollins drops both hands to his sides, palms pointing down to his boots. He rises a few feet…just enough to look out into the floor above us.

I release a gasp. "I didn't know we could levitate ourselves."

Without turning back around, Rollins answers, "Just one of the many things I learned here." My brother sticks the barrel of his gun through the partial opening. He sweeps it back and forth a couple of times across the floor. "I'll tell you what…if we make it out of here"—he looks back at me—"I'll teach you how to do this. Come on; the coast is clear."

Rollins climbs out onto the deserted floor, checking up and down the hall again before pulling both Ria and me up.

"Did you have to shoot her?" I ask my brother. My eyes find Ria on the floor. Her eyes remain closed and she appears to be fast asleep.

"I just zapped her," he says, like it's no big deal, before picking her up. "She'll be fine. Friend of yours?" He checks behind himself again before moving toward the door at the end of the hall.

"Yeah, something like that." I think back to the plane again. "We were both taken at the same time, along with a couple of her friends. I guess they're still here somewhere."

A little blue camera blinks at us from over the catwalk's door. Rollins swipes his access card and there's an immediate click. He pulls down on the handle; the door remains locked. He anxiously scans his card again—same results.

"They must've deactivated my card."

I look up at my brother and wait for him to come up with a plan. His eyes move down the hall. I know he has something.

"Come on."

We rush down the hallway, sliding back into the stuck elevator. Once we're in, Rollins lifts up both of his hands and removes the elevator hatch in the ceiling. The square steel door flies off and clangs to the side.

Rollins, again, levitates himself up through the opening, sticking only his head out before continuing all the way out. He sends for Ria and me—the three of us are now on the roof of the elevator.

I look around. A large cable, not even half as thick as the ones connected to the drones, holds the three of us suspended in the air, along with the thousand pound elevator underneath our feet. With each step Rollins takes, the elevator sways an inch or so back and forth.

I glance up. The top floor is maybe twenty yards away. I don't want to look down, but force myself to anyway. The darkness swallows up whatever's below.

There's a loud click, and the elevator shifts down a couple of feet.

"Either they just turned the power back on or this thing's about to drop." My knees feel weak. Shaky. I lower myself to the ground and squat next to Ria. Her eyes are still shut; a deadpan expression paints her face. I stare down into hole at the elevator's insides. It's still stuck halfway between the two floors, but it's moved down noticeably. The lights flicker on in the cabin, answering my own question.

Rollins notices the lights shining down by his feet, too. "Time to go. Grab hold of my shoulder." He then lifts Ria up with ease, throwing her over his free shoulder. His hands fall to his sides and he levitates the three of us off the roof of the elevator.

About halfway to the top of the shaft, the elevator below clicks on, the sound echoing through the darkness. Ria moves her head to the side, waking up. Her body is hanging limp upside down, eyes focusing on the steel box rising up.

She tenses up.

"Ahhhhhhhh!" A confused Ria screams, overtaking any noises

coming from the climbing elevator at our heels. She turns her head and notices me on the other side for the first time.

I glance over at her and reach out for her hand. She squeezes it back, refusing to let go.

The elevator continues to climb, now only a couple of floors away.

She closes her mouth and then her eyes. I look down—the steel death box seems to be gaining speed. Whoever is in control is trying to flatten us with it. I glance back up. We're almost to the top. Maybe one or two more levels to go.

Rollins chokes out a surprised yelp when the elevator strikes the heels of his feet.

We leap off to the side, the three of us crashing onto a small cement ledge just off the top floor. The elevator continues its mission and plows into the ceiling. An array of electrical sparks flash on impact. The roof of the elevator folds in, destroyed. I turn to the side, staring at the bottom of an unpainted door. I reach up and pull down on the handle.

It's locked.

I lift my palm up and pull the handle clear off the door, creating an entrance. I can't let Ria see Rollins do everything.

We step into the next room, the lab I was in earlier, which leads out into the drone hangar.

The three of us walk in a clump, with Rollins in the lead. He holds his gun out in front of him. Two doctors talk in the far corner of the lab, while both busily study a tablet in front of them. We get close enough to spy what they are discussing. Individual photos of the three of us fill the screen. The words *Wanted* and *Dangerous* scream back from where we observe.

"Hey!" my brother shouts, getting their attention.

Startled, both men jump, searching for the unknown voice.

Rollins lifts his gun and aims it at the doctor holding the tablet. He fires a single shot. The man drops to the floor. The tablet falls from his hands, the screen cracking on impact. Rollins trains the gun on the lone man still on his feet.

"You," he calls out, "which one of these Eagles is fully charged?"

The doctor nervously looks down at his lifeless friend before forcing his attention back up at Rollins and then onto the end of the gun. His hand points to an aerial drone to his right, still connected to its steel plate in the ceiling.

"You're never going to escape," the man mutters. He eyes shift over to Ria and then me. "Aren't you the kid who tried to run the other day? You saw what happened."

I tap Rollins on the shoulder from behind. "He's right. There's some kind of invisible electrical fence surrounding this place. It's impossible to get out of here."

At first, Rollins doesn't respond. His eyes are focused on the drone about ten yards away from the doctor before a serendipitous smile forms on his face. "I don't plan on going through the wall, little bro. We're gonna fly over it."

CHAPTER 24

ESCAPE PLAN

"Get us in the air," Rollins commands, seated behind the controls in the ShadowEagle drone. Ria and I are squeezed into the seat behind Rollins and watch him bark out orders to the doctor, who is frantically hitting buttons on a new tablet. The barrel to Rollins's gun sticks halfway out of the open canopy of the aircraft, aimed at the back of the man's head.

"Freeze!" A group of voices yell at us from across the floor. A large group of Tele soldiers rush toward us, guns already drawn. "Exit the drone!"

Rollins turns toward the voices and fires multiple shots in their direction, pushing them back. "Get us in the air, *now,*" he screams at the doctor. "I'm tired of playing games with you!"

The doctor steps over his friend still lying on the floor. He glances back at us before entering something onto the screen. His typed command into the tablet shoots blue flames out the back of our aircraft and our seats begin to vibrate. A series of loud clicks rings out over us sending the overhead steel plate in motion. Sunlight begins to squeeze through the increasing narrow opening to illuminate the body of the drone.

Shots are fired in our direction; one striking the side of the canopy inches away from Ria's head. She ducks as she holds her arm across her face. Her loose hand finds mine in my lap, squeezing it tight.

Rollins trains his gun back toward the group of soldiers and

116

begins to fire off a series of erratic shots in their direction, buying us some time.

I glance up. The circular plate is about halfway open.

"Close the canopy," Rollins calls out to the doctor between shots. Bullets fly over his head, forcing him to duck.

"Ahhhh," Ria cries out. "I've been hit!"

My eyes jump from the ceiling down to Ria's shirt. A small growing red stain has suddenly appeared on the sleeve of her outer shoulder. A stream of blood trickles down her arm. "Rollins!" I clench my teeth. "Get us outta here."

My brother blindly fires his gun a few more times across the hangar as the canopy closes, sealing us into the cockpit. He turns and meets the tears in Ria's eyes. More bullets strike the drone, ricocheting off the bulletproof protective body all around us.

"I don't wanna die! I don't wanna die!"

The black tubing—the drone's power source—detaches itself from the Hawk and the blue flames in the rear of the ship shift downward, slowly lifting us out of the hole.

"Here," Rollins says. He passes me a large hunting knife from his belt—reminding me of the one I discovered on the plane. "Cut your shirt up and wrap it tightly around her arm. You gotta apply pressure to slow the bleeding."

I do as my brother instructed, while the drone continues its climb off the launching pad. Shots are fired from below, hitting the floorboard, but all harmlessly bouncing off the bottom of the aircraft.

"Any idea how to fly this thing?" I ask Rollins, while tying the strip of cloth around Ria's arm.

She winces and closes her eyes.

I place my arm around her and pull her in, careful not to touch her wound.

Rollins is checking out the small control panel in front of him. He pushes a button labeled MANUAL, which causes the drone to start shaking before tipping slightly forward. He grabs hold of the lever between his knees and pulls back, balancing us out. "It's just like a flight simulator. They trained us on these back when I first arrived at the Compound."

We continue our climb into the air and we get a full view of the dense land below. Green forest extends outward in every direction I look, until all I see is the blue ocean surrounding it.

"We were on an island?" I question, relieved to be leaving this place.

*   *   *

In the short time we've been in the air, Ria's entire arm is now covered in red. Her head is tipped back to the side, leaning halfway off the seat's headrest behind her. Her eyes are closed, but her hand still grips the piece of cloth wrapped around her shoulder. Every few minutes, she yelps out in pain.

Rollins turns his head. "If we don't get her to a doctor soon, your friend there is gonna bleed out."

I nod my head, already thinking this. "Where are we gonna find someone who's willing help us?"

"The only other place we know," Rollins quickly answers, his eyes searching for something outside of the canopy. Below us, the dark blue ocean slowly begins to fade into a massive gray land. "Sol."

*   *   *

As we approach our old sector, we begin to descend from the clouds. Rollins glides us smoothly over buildings and rooftops as he looks for a safe place to land. We come across an old, abandoned neighborhood on the north side of Sol that a fire took out years ago.

"I've never been out here before." I gaze out both sides of the darkly tinted canopy—burned down houses line the road with not a single working vehicle in sight.

"We can't risk getting caught. This neighborhood's empty." Rollins steers the drone down the road, only a few inches over the pothole-filled pavement as we search for a safe place to hide the Eagle. We whisk by a small stretch of houses, all still erect and untouched by the fire. "Plus, there's a hospital just over the hill. Your friend doesn't look good."

I glance over at Ria; her head lays across my chest. Her skin is ashen, covered in sweat. I pull back her bangs and hook them behind her ear. Her eyes remain closed.

Rollins parks the drone between two intact houses.

"We may get lucky and find a first aid kit or something inside."

Ria lets out a gasp as I levitate her out of the drone. The entire right side of her shirt is now stained red, her hand still holding the soaked rag against her arm.

We walk up to the front door, Rollins loosely holding his gun to

118

the side. He reaches out for the handle, but the door opens on its own, as if the owner of the house was waiting for us to arrive. The barrel end of a double-barrel shotgun protrudes out before Rollins has a chance to react.

"Woo-hoo! What do we have here?" An old lady stands square in the doorway, cackling. She holds the tip of her shotgun inches away from the center of Rollins's chest. "Looks like Christmas came early this year."

CHAPTER 25

HOSPITAL

"Tie him up to that chair," the old woman orders me. She shifts her gun over at Rollins. "There's some rope in that closet over there." The gray-haired woman wears khaki pants, a flowered shirt, and a sun hat. Her clothes make it appear as if she was gardening outside when we arrived.

I retrieve the rope from the closet and begin tying up my brother in a chair facing a tattered couch. The house has an awful smell to it—a combination of boiled cabbage and dirty feet mixed together. I glance around the room. *So this is where it all ends, huh?* The living room is painted mustard yellow with a few framed family photographs hanging off the walls around us. All the furniture in the living room seems to be outdated by at least twenty or thirty years.

"I can't stand you Government people always coming around, bothering me on my property. Telling me what to do, how to think—"

"Lady," Rollins begins, "like I said, our friend is hurt bad. We're just here looking for some bandages and maybe some—"

"Yeah, I've fallen for the injured card before," she cuts him off. "If you're not part of the Government's Army, then what's with the uniforms? And the patches?" The surly woman uses the end of her shotgun to motion toward the patch of the blackbird with red stars for eyes sewn on both of our sleeves—the operation's symbol.

"If we were Government, you'd already be dead," I snap. I've lost my patience with the woman. I turn and stand up from the squatting position behind Rollin's chair. "If you're not going to help us, then please just let us go." An image of Ria flashes through my head. The old woman forced us to leave her outside on the steps.

"We'll see about that," the old woman says, approaching Rollins in the chair. She holds out the shotgun between the two of them and sticks him in his midsection with the tip of the barrel. "I have friends who'd pay top dollar for some kids like you." She continues to probe Rollin's stomach with the end of her gun. "And in such good shape, too."

My knees tremble, and I get a sick feeling in the back of my throat.

The woman shifts toward me. "You—toss me that rope down there by your feet and then have a seat in the chair."

The woman props her gun up next to her, placing it barrel up against the wall, only an arm's length away. I pick up the rope without a word and throw it over to the woman. She miscalculates it, the coiled rope landing in a pile at her feet.

The woman shoots me a dirty look before bending down to pick it up in front of her.

Here's my chance.

I lift my palm out and send the shotgun flying across the room and into my hands before the old lady even has a chance to react. I pump the gun, aiming the weapon at the woman's chest.

"You're Teles?" her frightened voice drops. Shaking, she sits on the couch behind her and allows the rope to fall from her hands.

"Nic, untie me," Rollins says, sounding aggravated. "And tie up that old bat. I'm gonna get Ria off the porch."

I rush over to him and free my brother before tying up the old lady with both pieces of rope.

"You can't just leave me here like this," the woman pleads, as I secure her hands behind the chair. "Take whatever you want. It's all yours!"

"Oh, we plan to," Rollins brings Ria into the living room and places her on the couch. She lets out another groan, coughing up a trickle of blood.

"We've gotta get her to the hospital." I stare down at her. I wipe away a small trail of blood from the side of her mouth with the corner of my torn shirt. If it's even possible, her skin has turned a shade paler. She looks like she hasn't seen the sun in years.

Rollins rushes back into the living room holding a box of bandages and a black plastic bottle of some kind of ointment in his hands. He pushes me out of the way and tears off the sleeve of Ria's shirt, exposing her gunshot wound. Blood squirts out of the hole as soon as he removes the red-stained soaked cloth from her shoulder.

"That girl needs a blood transfusion," the old lady says, with a worried look from across the room. "You're not going to help her with some bandages and ointment. She needs a doctor."

Rollins ignores her and squeezes the bottle's contents out onto Ria's shoulder, the ointment cascading down her arm and onto the couch.

Ria immediately cries out in pain, the upper half of her body sprouting up. Her eyes shoot open, but only for a second or two before she relaxes back on the couch and drifts off into another deep sleep.

Rollins then takes the strips of gauze and wraps them around her arm and shoulder, using all of the bandages in the box. The thin white cloth bleeds through, confirming what the old woman just said.

"Grab my gun and let's go," Rollins says, levitating Ria. She winces in pain again, as her body hovers in the air a couple of feet off the couch.

"Please," the old lady begs again. "Please, don't leave me tied up like this!"

The three of us exit the small house; neither Rollins nor I looks back.

*   *   *

The parking lot in front of the hospital is not even halfway filled with vehicles. Only the rich can afford to go to a hospital when they are sick, so the place is pretty empty.

"They're gonna arrest us as soon as we set foot into the place." I eye the front doors from where we crouch down behind a car in the parking lot. On either side of the hospital's entrance, a FootSoldier drone stands at attention. Each drone holds an automatic gun across his chest, not at all inviting.

"Correct. That's why we're gonna cause a diversion and walk right through those front doors as if we own the place." Rollins looks off to the side where he placed Ria. "We need to get in there and find a Healer. All hospitals have them now."

I nod, gripping the shotgun in my hands before glancing down at Ria. "Let's do this."

Rollins turns and looks around behind us, searching for something. His eyes find a small black car parked a few rows back in the parking lot all by itself. He raises his hand, instantly lifting the vehicle off the ground. The black car careens up in the air, my brother's hand mirroring it as it soars up, gaining altitude as if gravity no longer existed.

I turn back to the entrance and watch one of the drones radio in what they're seeing. They then leave their post, stiffly sprinting across the parking lot right past us.

The car continues its climb, almost to the point now where I can't even see it anymore.

"That should do," Rollins says calmly. He drops his arm to his side. "Come on." The car pauses in midair for a second or two before plummeting back down to earth at an alarming rate. It lands in a fiery explosion at the feet of the two FootSoldier drones. Rollins doesn't even turn back to admire his creation.

And just like my brother said, we waltz right through the front doors, like we own the place—until Rollins lifts up his gun, shoving it into the face of the receptionist announcing our arrival.

CHAPTER 26

THE HEALER

"Drop the phone, now," Rollins roars, as he shoves the end of his gun in the receptionist's face. "Get us a doctor!" He places Ria on a nearby empty gurney in the hospital lobby.

"Sir, there's no need…" The woman peeks around the side of my brother and discovers her security is missing from the entrance before changing her tune. "I'll call someone up right now."

The woman reaches for the phone again, and Rollins shoves the gun even closer to her face, forcing her to release her grip on the Receiver.

"What—do you think we're stupid?" Rollins calls out, his voice rising even louder. "You'll have a dozen FootSoldiers here before any doctor shows up. Just point us in the right direction. We'll take it from there."

The woman's trembling hand points down the hall. "Down through the double doors is the ER."

"See, that wasn't so hard, now was it?" Rollins takes a quick glance over his shoulder at the entrance. He then flips his gun around and brings the butt of the weapon down hard, striking the receptionist's forehead. The woman slumps over in her chair and falls to the ground. She's knocked out cold. "Can't take any chances."

Someone coughs behind us in the corner, followed by a muttered curse word.

I jump and turn around, discovering we have company. "What

about them?" I motion behind us with the end of the shotgun.

Rollins spins and eyes a man and a woman huddled up in the corner of the lobby. The woman holds a hand over her mouth, her face pale and covered in sweat. Her eyes are glued to the linoleum floor in front of her. She refuses to make eye contact with either of us. The man stands before her and shields his wife from our view. Other than the couple, the place is deserted.

"You two…get on your feet and get over here!" Rollins waves the gun around the lobby like he's a madman. The couple scurries over to us, as the man helps his wife across the floor. The woman releases another loud cough, choking back tears.

"Let's move," Rollins says. He cues me to grab Ria's gurney. "We'll have company before we know it."

The couple moves ahead of us and leads the way down the hall to the Emergency Room entrance. The man is young, maybe in his early thirties, dressed in a shirt and tie. His partner appears to be around the same age, but is dressed like she looks—like the plague hit her. Her faded, raggedy bathrobe hangs off her body. She keeps one hand over her chronic cough, while her free hand holds her robe together.

The man turns back. He eyes Rollins first and then me.

"Keep your eyes forward," I shout, before Rollins can order him to do the same.

Rollins's expression is deadpan as he glances over at me. He gives me a single nod of approval.

The couple leads us through the doors of the ER. Partitions separate the area into private cubicles with walls so low you can see all the way across the large room. Only a handful of patients are scattered around in single beds, each hooked up to a monitor of some kind.

"Hey, Doc!" Rollins calls out. He holds the gun vertically so everyone can see it. "Get over here and help our friend. She's been shot."

A middle-aged man dashes across the floor to grab Ria's gurney. He glances up, his eyes flashing over to the sick woman we took hostage standing behind us. His head tilts to the side as he tries to put all of the pieces together.

A nurse rushes up with a wheelchair. "What about her?" The nurse points to our sick hostage, who leans on her husband.

"Yeah, she needs help, too," I answer quickly, before Rollins can say otherwise. My brother flashes me a look of discontent before turning his attention back to the doctor.

Ria lets out another groan as she's wheeled over to a nearby empty cubicle.

"What happened to this young lady?" The doctor tries to sound calm, but every few seconds he glances back at one of the guns and trembles.

"She was shot in the shoulder. What does it look like?" Rollins grips his weapon tighter across his chest. "Get her in the Healer."

The doctor turns around confused. "Son, Healers are extremely expensive. We can't afford—"

My brother doesn't even let him finish. He straightens out his gun and zaps the doctor in the chest. No blood spews out, but the man lays unconscious on the floor.

"What did you do that for?" I scream. "Now what are we gonna do?"

The nurse rushes over to the doctor and squats down on one knee to check his pulse.

Rollins ignores me and presses his gun up against the nurse's temple. "Now, let's try this again. Where's the Healer?"

The nurse pushes herself up and points to the back of the room. "In the last cubicle, by the door." She looks like she's about to faint.

Rollins floats Ria across the room. He places her in something that looks like a tanning bed.

The Healer.

"Get over here and turn this thing on," my brother orders the nurse. "Or you're next." He wipes away a thin layer of sweat from his forehead before placing his finger back on the trigger.

The nurse scuttles over to us and begins to hit a series of buttons on the coffin-like device. She keeps her head down, eyes on the screen the entire time. The lid of the device closes. Ria is secured inside. The machine begins to rumble, emitting a loud humming noise.

My eyes shoot from Rollins to the nurse. I wonder if it's a good sign.

A loud, booming cough discharges behind us.

Both Rollins and I turn to see the woman down, both knees on the floor. The wheelchair is positioned behind her. Her husband holds his arm across her back as she releases another series of dry coughs.

"She needs help," the man cries out. "She's been like this for almost a week now, and it's only getting worse."

"As soon as we're done, the machine's all yours," Rollins says calmly. He eyes the woman on the floor.

Rollins and I turn back around to discover a timer counting down from twenty minutes.

"We don't have that kind of time," Rollins mutters out loud. He turns toward me. "Go grab the keys off the lady at the front desk. Secure the front doors."

I grip the shotgun with both hands, hurling myself through the ER doors and down the hallway back to the entrance. I snatch the keys off the desk and dart for the door. As soon as I place the small key in the keyhole, a FootSoldier comes in view rushing toward the glass.

I turn the key just as the drone halts about ten feet away from the entrance.

It aims and fires its gun.

Boom!

CHAPTER 27

NO ESCAPE

I drop the shotgun at my feet and lift up both hands before me just in time. I concentrate on the bullets rocketing toward me and try to slow them down. They spray across the door, but the glass doesn't break. The door appears to have absorbed the bullets, freezing them.

I drop my hands, shocked that it even worked. The FootSoldier takes off for the side of the building and is joined by three other drones from the parking lot.

I double back across the hospital lobby and keep running until I reach the end of the hallway and cross back through the double doors of the ER.

"Drones tried to shoot through the glass," I say out of breath, "but I…"

The male hostage is standing stiffly behind Rollins, both of their backs to me. The man is holding up something shiny in front of my brother's face. He halfway turns his head at the sound of my voice. He has my brother's knife pressed up against the edge of Rollins's throat just below the chin.

"Get her out of the Healer," the man bellows out. He yanks Rollins over to where his wife lays unconscious on the floor. "Can't you see she's dying?" He shoves Rollins down on his knees, so he's only inches away from the curled-up woman's face.

The nurse stands by the Healer, frozen, unsure what to do.

"Drop the gun, now," the man calls out to me, not even looking up. His brown eyes shift back and forth between his wife and me.

I drop the shotgun to my feet, lifting both hands. As soon as the man looks away, I reach out and slip the knife right out of his hands. The sharp weapon flies over to me before the man even has a clue of what happened.

He releases his hold on Rollins, which allows my brother to pick up the gun at his feet.

"You're a Tele?"

No one answers the man, so he hurries over to his lifeless wife, picking her up and placing her back into the wheelchair.

"I tried, honey. I really did." The man leans over to whisper into her ear. His tie has been loosened; tears are running down his face. "I'm so, so sorry."

The timer is still counting down on the Healer; now less than ten minutes remain.

"See if you can find another exit," Rollins calls over to me. "We've gotta figure a way outta here."

I hand Rollins his knife before picking up the shotgun. I exit the ER again, taking a different hallway that leads deeper into the middle of the building. I come across a door labeled EMERGENCY EXIT. I push in on the handle and bright sunlight sneaks in from outside.

A handful of FootSoldiers rush the open door, all five of them holding up their guns. Without warning, they release multiple shots, drilling the outside of the door as soon as I seal off the exit.

I move even farther into the empty building, not coming across another emergency exit until the next hall down. I hesitantly push open the door, only to see a group of three Hawks soaring across the sky toward the hospital. A pair of FootSoldiers spot me from a short distance away and rush toward the temporary opening, forcing me to close them off.

There's pounding on the door behind me, mechanical voices ordering me to open up.

We're surrounded.

Instead of moving even deeper into the hospital, I head back to the ER. I fly through the double doors just as the nurse is opening the lid to the Healer. Rollins, along with the nurse and the man all stand around the machine staring at an unconscious Ria.

I rush up to the group and push my way forward, forgetting the mess we're in. I grab Ria's hand. Her eyes flicker, opening for the first time since back at the old lady's house. An enormous smile spreads across her face.

"So that's what it feels like to be rich," she says still glowing.

Still holding her hand, I lift her up in the machine. She winces and grabs at her shoulder. The bullet hole has healed, but her skin is still stained red from all of the blood.

"Did it work?"

She slowly sits up and rotates the ball of her arm around in her shoulder, moving it clockwise before reversing it. "I think it's just really sore."

"We've gotta go," Rollins says. He grabs me by the back of the shoulder. "Find a way out?"

"The place is surrounded." My eyes drop. "I think the entire Government's Army is out there waiting for us."

Rollins straps his headgear back on and picks up his gun. "There's gotta be a way. Let's move!"

We leave the man and his wife in the ER with the nurse...they can't assist us any more than they already have. Rollins is leading the way down one hallway to the next as if he's been here before and knows the escape route.

We come across an exit that reads: STAIRWAY TO PARKING GARAGE.

Rollins darts through the door, and we find a staircase leading underground. The three of us rush down the stairs in a single-file line, taking two stairs at a time.

Rollins pulls on the handle just as the door flies open, almost smacking him in the face. A man stands before us, dressed in all white with the initials EMT stitched onto the pocket of his scrubs. The expression on his face tells me he's just as surprised to see us as we are by him.

My brother digs the end of his gun into the man's chest and pushes him back out through the door. The man presses himself up against the outside wall, while trying to make himself as small as possible.

"Please don't shoot! Please don't shoot!" His hands are over his head, reaching for the cement ceiling above him.

Rollins shoves the man down on the ground with the barrel of his gun. A group of four ambulances are parked in a row, all backed into parking spots in front the exit. A few other cars are scattered across the indoor parking garage.

I rush over to the nearest ambulance and peer in through the closed window. A set of keys dangles down from the ignition.

"I know that symbol tattooed on the back of your neck," the man says to Rollins, now looking up at him.

"Yeah? What do you know?"

"Come on." I smack Rollins on the arm. "The keys are in the first one."

My brother ignores me, as he glares at the man. "I said, what do you know?"

"I know someone who can help you." The man dressed in all white looks over at the line of ambulances. "I can take you to him."

Rollins stares over at the man, weighing the decision.

I look down at the opposite end of the garage toward the exit, before trotting back to my brother. "Come on. Rollins. We have to go. There are drones all over the place."

"He's coming with us." Rollins pulls the man to his feet by his shirtsleeve.

The four of us climb into the front cab of the ambulance; my brother takes the wheel. He cranks up the engine and places his gun across the dashboard in front of him.

As the vehicle lurches forward, I grip the end of the shotgun in my hands, holding it securely between my legs. I look over at Ria and produce a weak smile, assuring her it will all be okay—even though I'm not so sure myself.

She leans over and gives me a light kiss on the cheek.

Suddenly, all of my worries wash away.

CHAPTER 28

AMBULANCE RIDE

We barrel through the parking garage, the ambulance heading for the gated exit up ahead. Rollins grips the steering wheel, not taking his foot off the gas. The parking lot dips down as we approach the gate.

"Better stop up here," says the man wedged in-between Rollins and me. "We'll have drones on us in seconds if you just fly through it."

A red-and-white-striped pole comes into view, blocking the exit. Rollins grits his teeth as he slams on the brakes. The ambulance comes to a roaring stop and slides up to the gate. The uniformed man at the helm glances over at us lethargically. His hand is already on the button that raises the gate. A puzzled expression grows over his face.

"I don't know you," he says. The man straightens up and looks Rollins up and down, before shifting over to the EMT sitting between us. "Sully?" The gatekeeper tilts his head. "What's going on here?"

"We're just taking this one out for...maintenance," Sully lies, staring back at the man. He wipes a stream of sweat off the side of his face. "Hot one out today, yeah?" He laughs nervously to himself.

The man's eyes shift back to Rollins before falling onto me and then Ria.

"What's with the kids?"

"Oh, they're just"—Sully digs for another lie—"my son and his friends. He wanted to see what his old man does every day." Again, he follows up the lie with a nervous chuckle.

The garage attendee processes the information and lifts his hand to open the gate, but then freezes. His eyebrows scrunch down. "Wait, Sully. You don't have any—"

Rollins floors it. The ambulance rams through the barrier, breaking the pole right off its hinges. We peel around the corner and explode out onto the street that runs parallel to the front of the building.

Multiple Hawks fill the sky over the roof and parking lot of the hospital. All four of us look out of the windows examining them. Up ahead, FootSoldier drones have blocked off the road, searching any vehicles attempting to go through.

"Take a left up here," Sully says. He points to an unmarked side road. "And then take another left. That should get us around them."

We all stare at the roadblock as we turn off the main road and onto a side street.

That was way too simple. These people are not going to give up on us that easily.

We take the upcoming left and are turning onto the next road when an unexpected force plows into the side of the ambulance spinning the back end of the vehicle around, sliding us across the narrow side street. The ambulance flips over on its side jamming the four of us all down on top of each other in the cab.

"Is everyone okay?" I groan and try to lift myself up. The top half of my body is forced up against Ria, who's crammed face-first up against the passenger side. The road stares back at her from the other side of the unbroken glass. Sully is sprawled across the dashboard, along with Rollins, who is wedged up against Sully and me.

No one moves, but one by one everyone releases a moan, some louder than others.

"Wait, wait!" I say, scrunching down my eyebrows. "Listen."

The sound of multiple car doors closing rings out behind us. A feeling of panic engulfs the cab.

"FootSoldiers!" I gasp out.

Unsure of what to do, no one says anything for a few seconds. We hear loud mechanical noises behind us, so we know the drones are approaching the side of the ambulance that is flipped up.

"Everyone through here," Rollins says. He wrestles open a small, stuck window that leads to the rear of the ambulance.

The rectangular window gives, sliding open a couple of feet. I can tell by just looking at it that there's no way I'll be able to squeeze through the small opening.

I switch places with Ria and help her up to the window first before she easily climbs through it. Rollins hands both of the guns to her through the narrow opening as soon as she's on the other side. Next goes Sully, who I just now realize has a small laceration across the center of his forehead from where his head must have struck the windshield. A small stream of blood trickles down his nose and cheek. As soon as he's on the other side, he wipes away at the cut across his face.

"You're up next, little bro."

I shake my head as I study the opening again. "There's no way I can squeeze through that." I keep my voice down so Ria doesn't hear—like she doesn't already know I'm overweight.

"Well," Rollins begins in a calm voice, "you can either stay here and get shot, arrested, or both—or try to squeeze yourself through the window. It's up to you." Rollins's eyes flash from me to the driver's side mirror. Multiple black figures come into view.

"You first," I say to Rollins. I glance back at the approaching drones in the mirror. "I think I have a plan."

Rollins flips around and squeezes himself headfirst through the window. His wide shoulders almost prevent him from fitting through, but with a big push from behind, he falls out on the other side.

Boom!

The rearview mirror explodes off the side of the ambulance.

"Hand me the shotgun," I whisper, holding my hand through the open window.

Without question, someone places the heavy weapon in my hand. I cock it back. "Cover your ears. This is gonna be loud."

Boom!

A thunderous explosion rings through the cab, the force from the gun ramming my shoulder and back up against the passenger side window behind me. The driver's side window shatters above me and glass spouts out of the cab like a fountain. As soon as it breaks, the drones react with an immediate follow-up attack of their own. Their guns light up the side of the ambulance, spraying holes all over the body of the vehicle.

"They think we're shooting at them," I yell out. Just as I was hoping, the body of the vehicle shields us from the attack. We're bulletproof—for now.

I throw my arms through the window leading to the back of the ambulance and begin inching my body through the small opening. I bring my shoulders together just like Rollins did, making myself as minuscule as possible. Once I'm through, I pick up the shotgun. I double cock it this time before firing off two more rounds through the cab. The entire windshield, almost still intact, flies off the front of the ambulance as the second shot rings out.

The FootSoldier drones echo the shots with more gunfire of their own as they make their way to the front of the cab. We hear the driver's side door creak open, which gives us the signal to jump out the back.

"You are all under arrest..." We hear a mechanical voice start in the front cab before going silent. The FootSoldier realizes it has just been fooled.

The four of us climb into the military Humvee parked behind the ruined ambulance. Rollins, again, is behind the wheel. He presses in the ignition button; the engine rumbles. The small group of FootSoldiers all turn at the same time, putting the pieces together. Simultaneously, they raise their weapons. Rollins shifts down the gear and flings the vehicle into reverse, jolting us backward. We build up speed, putting distance between the ambulance and us as bullets spray across our windshield. Everyone ducks but Rollins. The window, just like the body of the Humvee, appears to be bulletproof.

Once Rollins decides we have gone far enough in reverse, with a flip of his wrist, he spins the military truck around, racing us down the road and away from the hospital and drones.

CHAPTER 29

HELP

By the time we pull into the driveway, stars have already begun to blanket the sky over us. The full moon shines and illuminates the small farmhouse close to the main road. An old, defunct dirt field lies behind the house, appearing unable to grow anything green in quite some time.

"This used to be an old orange tree grove decades ago," Sully informs us as we climb out of the Humvee. "But I didn't bring you here for fruit."

My stomach grumbles at the mention of food. An orange would be unbelievably good right now. I think back to my last meal at the Compound this morning—lumpy oatmeal with raisins sprinkled over the top. Even that mush would be welcome at this point.

After a heated discussion, Sully convinces us to leave the guns in the Humvee, so we don't startle his friend. He agrees to allow Rollins to keep his knife, which eases my brother's mind, before leading the way up the short staircase and onto the porch, knocking on the screen door.

Almost a full minute later, the front door creaks open. A slender man with short gray hair, wearing a white T-shirt and khakis, greets us holding the door halfway open. He pushes his thin wired-framed glasses up his nose; his muddled eyes study us through the screen door. His wrist is bare, unlike Sully, who still wears a Receiver.

"Sully!" The man's face lights up when he recognizes the EMT still in his uniform. "Do you know what time it is? Is everything okay?"

Sully nods his head a few times before standing off to the side. "Doc, let me introduce you to some friends of mine—Rollins, Nic, and Ria." Sully then leans in toward the man, whispering, "They're from the Compound."

A grave look flits over the man's face. He pushes the screen door out and takes a single step onto the porch. The man looks in both directions, his eyes shifting back and forth, checking to see if we were followed. His gaze lands back on Sully. "And you brought them here? Did you already disable your Tracker?" His voice jumps.

He nods his head and pulls a tiny microchip out of his front pocket. His Receiver is powered off. "They're in trouble. I told them you might be able to help."

The man closes his eyes for a second. He ponders the situation before exhaling. With a sharp nod, he says, "Come on," as if he really doesn't have another option.

The man opens up the screen door the rest of the way and allows us to enter single file. He grabs Rollins's arm as he tries to pass, hooking him in the crook. He squints as he examines the marking on the back of his neck. "So you're all Teles?"

Rollins's nod answers for the group. The man releases his grip on my brother's arm, but I can feel his eyes studying the tattoo on the back of my neck as I pass into his house.

The man sits in a recliner facing the large beat-up couch the three of us sit on. His eyes scan us back and forth waiting for someone to speak.

"Kids, this is Doc," Sully yells from the other room. He attempts to break the tension. "He's someone you can trust."

My eyes search for Sully's voice and land on a lone painting hanging off the wall. It's so dim in here I can't tell if it's a painting of a flower or a boat. Family photos are noticeably absent.

"I used to be a lab doctor at the Compound a few years ago." Doc decides to break his silence.

My whole body tenses at the very mention of the facility, my eyes finding the front door. I have a strange feeling about all of this.

"Calm down...calm down." Doc sounds almost a little agitated at my sudden change in body language. "I hate them as much as you all do." He shifts his attention to my brother. "What do you know about the tattoo on the back of your neck?"

Rollins scoots up to the edge of the old couch. "I know they install something in our heads that gives them the power to control us." He answers the question as if this is common knowledge, no big deal.

"You're correct," he says like the host of a game show. "We called it a Wash." As if it's a nervous habit, Doc uses his index finger to slide his glasses up again, even though they rest high on his nose. "There's also a built-in Tracker in the tattoo, so they know your whereabouts at all times."

Rollins starts to push himself up off the couch before Doc holds his hand out to stop him.

"But being this far away from the Compound, they shouldn't be able to determine your exact location any time soon."

Ria and I shift back in our seats, but Rollins stays tensed, back straight—stiff.

"But we do need to get them out of you as soon as possible. Their technology could've improved since I left."

Sully walks back into the living room. He carries a plate full of some kind of sliced dark meat and crackers. "Didn't have much to pick from, but I know you kids are hungry." He places it in the center of the coffee table that separates the couch from the recliner.

My eyes study the food on the plate. Do I eat it? The food could be poisoned. I think back to the old lady whose shotgun I now possess. She talked about how she was going to sell us to her friend. Maybe this guy is planning to drug us and do the same? But before I could talk myself out of it, I watch my hand reach for the plate, my stomach winning the debate.

"Who's first?" Doc asks, raising his eyebrows. "I have a lab setup in the back room."

Rollins stands and nods. He then turns toward me, lowering his shoulders and voice. "If anything happens, just get out of here. Okay?" He curls up the side of his mouth before turning and following the doctor out of the room. They head down a short hallway to the back of the house.

I slouch back on the couch to think about what Rollins just said. If he's having doubts about the doctor, too, why did he volunteer so willingly? I just got my brother back. I don't want to lose him again.

"So, what's the next move?" Sully questions Ria and me as soon as the three of us are alone in the room. He sits in the recliner across from the couch.

Down at the end of the hall I hear a door close and then lock. My eyes jump from the hallway back to Sully. I lift my shoulders. "Not sure." Even though this guy is helping us, I still don't fully trust him. I'll feel better when we get these things out of the back of our necks.

After about ten minutes, Doc wheels an unconscious Rollins into a neighboring room and closes the door behind him. He exits seconds later to let us know the procedure was a success. "Your brother's recovering nicely. Who's next?"

Ria pushes herself off the couch and volunteers to go second. She follows the doctor back down the hall, leaving just me and Sully in the living room.

"See, didn't I tell you Doc's a good guy?"

I nod my head, halfway accepting the idea they are here to help us.

Another ten minutes passes before Doc returns, ready to retrieve his last patient.

"Ready?" Doc looks me up and down. He pushes his glasses slightly up his nose again and waits for me to stand.

I follow the doctor down the hall and leave Sully by himself. I pass two closed doors on the way, presumably where Rollins and Ria are recovering. Doc opens the door at the end of the hallway. The only piece of furniture in the room is a chair, similar to a dentist's chair, but it has already been reclined to a flat surface.

"Lay down on your stomach," he says from behind me, putting on a pair of surgical gloves. "I need to keep you awake while we do this, so I can't give you anything for the pain."

I lie down in the reclined chair, glancing back at the doctor. "Pain?"

"It will only sting a bit at first." The doctor picks up a handheld chrome device off the small table next to him. The tool is in the shape of a handgun, but instead of a barrel it ends in a short point, like scissors.

I turn my head back and close my eyes. The cold tip of the gun-like device tickles the back of my neck before poking into my skin. A sharp pain rockets through my entire body as the tool burrows farther into my neck, attaching itself to something inside of me.

The doctor pulls back on the device and it feels like he's trying to yank my entire brain out of my head through a tiny hole. I grip onto both sides of the chair, praying it's almost over.

"Talk to me, Nic," Doc says. He leans over me. "It might take your mind off the pain." He pulls back on the device some more before burying it even farther into my neck.

I clench my teeth, unable to produce a single thought.

"You know, you're not the first from the island to find me." Doc gives up on me starting the conversation. "Another boy visited me a few months back. Kid had the strangest hairstyle...and a facial tattoo."

Kingston's eccentric red ponytail and chin tattoo comes to view. "Yeah?"

"Yeah, he'd escaped from the Compound just like you kids. He wanted the same procedure done on him."

"Did he say where he was headed?" I try to lift my head, but I'm paralyzed in the seat.

"The Metro, actually. You know, the old abandoned security building downtown?" The doctor stops a second to think. "Said there was something important there that he needed, but he couldn't be tracked. He said it would end everything."

I hear a loud suction noise behind me, followed by a single pop echoing through my head.

"All done."

CHAPTER 30

FARMHOUSE CELLAR

"Breaking news…another Tele attack in the Sol district today where two Teles viciously assaulted the children's ward at Sol's Sacred Hospital."

My eyes blink open to a news report beginning on an old television facing the couch. I look over. Both Rollins and Ria are wide awake sitting on opposite sides of me.

"As you can see in the video here, earlier today, brothers Rollins and Nicholas McCready levitated multiple cars in the hospital parking lot before launching them into the side of the building. We are getting word the children's ward was their target."

I watch the video play on the screen. It has clearly been altered, portraying us as perilous Tele murderers to the sector—all lies. Ria is nowhere to be seen in the video footage. Why would they edit her out? I look over at Rollins blankly. His eyes squint at the television, tense.

"We are still unsure how many children were harmed in the attack. This is the third Tele-related attack in the Sol district in the matter of days."

"Rollins?"

"As always, we're here to remind you"—a jingle begins—"if you see…something, say…something!

Headlights from a vehicle pulling into the driveway shine brightly in the front window. Doc and Sully rush back into the living room.

"Get into the back room," Doc orders us in a panicked voice. "I have a small storage cellar underneath the house that should be big enough to fit you three. The door's underneath the bed. Move!"

Both Ria and I wait for Rollins to react first. Could this be a trap? Rollins rushes down the hallway leading the way. We enter the room and find the door camouflaged in the floor.

One at a time, the three of us lower ourselves down the short ladder; Rollins goes last and pulls the door down, closing us in. Sully centers the bed back over the trapdoor before leaving the room.

The light clicks off, and we're left in the dark.

We hear the front door open in the other room. A mechanical voice booms out, "We are looking for Teles. Move aside, citizens."

"Now, wait a minute." Doc raises his voice to warn us. "You can't just walk in here—"

"Three Teles were tracked to this location. We need to search the house under direct orders from Commander Lee. You can make it easier on yourself if you inform us of their location now."

I hear the FootSoldiers turning over furniture in the living room.

"Explain the stolen Government vehicle parked out front." Loud, heavy footsteps trudge down the hall, getting closer to where we cower.

The bedroom door flies open and strikes the wall behind it. The overhead lamp clicks on; light shoots down through the cracks overhead surrounding the outline of the trap door. Ria's face glows. Her eyes find mine, telling me she's scared and wants me to hold her hand. I reach out just as the bed begins to slide over us, scraping loudly across the hardwood floor. More light sneaks in illuminating our hole.

"They're not here!" Doc raises his voice. "You're wasting your time."

"They were here," Sully adds. He forces the FootSoldier to halt the movement of the bed, "but they left!"

My hand wraps around Ria's. The ends of her fingernails graze the inside of my palm, lightly tickling me. I want to hold her so bad, make her feel safe and secure.

"Where to?" the mechanical voice doesn't get any louder, but sounds more intense.

"They held us at gunpoint and forced me to remove their Trackers," Doc says. "Then they left on foot, heading south."

Two quick shots ring out over us, followed by two heavy thumps on the floor. A few seconds later, we hear the front door slam shut and then the sound of multiple engines firing up in the driveway.

"I'm going up," Rollins says. He pushes on the trapdoor over us. "We need to assess the situation."

Rollins peeks the top half of his head just above the floor, before lifting the trapdoor all the way open. "They got Doc and Sully."

Rollins climbs out of the cellar, then helps Ria and me up. The bodies of our two innocent helpers lay across the bedroom floor. A small red dot is centered on both of their foreheads, trickling out two streams of blood.

The three of us step over the bodies and exit the room.

"Get whatever food and supplies you two can find." Rollins walks over to the front window in the living room and pulls back the see-through curtains. "Of course, they took the Humvee. I'm gonna try to find us some transportation."

Ria and I search the already overturned house, but like Sully said earlier, Doc really didn't have much food. I find an unloaded handgun in Doc's bedroom underneath his mattress, but other than that, the place is barren, as if the doctor hadn't lived here too long.

We walk outside looking for Rollins and discover him in the only other structure on the property—the dilapidated barn located next to the empty dirt field. He's sitting behind the wheel of an old truck, the dashboard already pulled free to show various colored wires underneath.

"Any luck?"

My brother ignores my question since he's busy pressing two different wires together, and after a moment the truck's engine roars to life. He taps his finger on the gas gauge over the steering wheel. "We're lucky this is an older model or I wouldn't have been able to hotwire it. Get in."

No one says a word about the two bodies lying on the floor inside the house, but I know we're all thinking about them as we pull away from the old farmhouse. If it wasn't for Sully and Doc, we would be the ones lying dead on the floor, not them.

CHAPTER 31

DEAD END

The truck jerks me awake as Rollins pulls into a parking spot a few blocks away from the Metro. I rub the sleep out of my eyes as I try to remember what my bed feels like at home—if I even have a home anymore. I picture my parents sitting at opposite ends at the dinner table. Did they search for me like they did for Rollins? Are they still searching for me? They're not the same people from a year ago, before my brother was taken.

Ria's hand covers mine between us on the seat and its touch brings me back to the cab in the truck. Her head rests against my shoulder, still sleeping.

"We're here," I whisper in her ear. My nose rubs up against the side of her neck. "Time to get up."

She wakes with a smile and stretches her arms out in front of her.

I glance over at Rollins. His hands still rest on the steering wheel. Two dark bags that were not there before hang under his eyes. He stares forward, looking at nothing in particular. Abandoned cars blanketed in dust line both sides of the street. Anti-Tele graffiti is plastered across the side of an old building facing us.

"It doesn't look like we were followed," Rollins says. He turns halfway around in his seat. "But you can't be too careful. Lee can have drones here in a matter of seconds."

My eyes wander across the street and I spot multiple active security cameras surveying the open road. I pull out three shirts I found in Doc's closet. "We can throw these on over our uniforms and disguise ourselves as homeless." Small groups of people huddle in various areas on both sides of the street surrounding the broken-down vehicles.

Rollins and Ria nod their agreement. They take the shirts and slip them on over their Tele uniforms.

"It's gonna be dawn soon," Rollins says. He looks up and out the front windshield. "We need to move."

The three of us exit the truck before smearing dirt across our faces and beginning our journey down the street. We creep across the trash-filled road using the shadows of the other tall downtown buildings surrounding us as protection. A loud humming noise fills the sky. A group of nearby homeless people sitting on the curb pops up, and they scatter in different directions. A bright spotlight clicks on over us and tears through the early morning's darkness. The three of us freeze, peering up and into the intense white light.

"Halt and identify yourself, citizens!" a loud, commanding, mechanical voice booms out of a speaker hidden in the light.

If we were still wearing our Receivers, we would have been identified instantly.

"Eagles!" I scream, even though Rollins and Ria didn't need the warning. "Run!"

We dart across the street and shoot down a narrow alley leading us to an immediate dead end. An abandoned skyscraper blocks our path, trapping us in.

I spin around in search of a way out. Multiple ShadowFlocks, along with dozens of ShadowEagle drones land, docking in the street about a hundred yards away from us. The alley is too narrow for them to land any closer. A small army of FootSoldiers pours out of the back of each of the ShadowFlocks, their matching eyes glowing a sinister red.

Ria screams, pointing at the Soldier drones charging at us from the street.

My brother produces his knife from his belt, but quickly re-sheaths it. The weapon is useless against machinery.

"Rollins, get us outta here!" I mirror Ria's scream. He's the only one of the three of us who can levitate ourselves.

"Not yet," he says, surprisingly calm. "We need to draw them in closer."

The growing number of FootSoldiers continues to march out of the landed oversized aerial drones in the street. More than half of them enter the mouth of the alley, allowing the others to stay back to guard the aircraft.

I spot an emergency fire escape ladder hanging down over a dumpster to the right of us. I get an idea. I lift up my palm and aim it at the ladder. Countless loud pops ring out and the steel bolts shoot off the wall it's connected to, freeing the twenty-foot ladder from the building. I swing the ladder around, sweeping it parallel to the ground at the charging group of drones. The makeshift weapon wipes out the entire frontline as it knocks back the FootSoldiers. I knew the force wouldn't stop them, only slow them down a bit, also making it appear we're fighting back.

The next group of drones sadistically marches over the already-fallen Soldiers as if they are not even there. Their red eyes glow brighter, piercing through the dark morning sky.

"Grab hold of my arms," Rollins says. "And don't let go."

The drones move closer, gripping their guns across their steel chests. The FootSoldiers who stayed back in the street abandon their posts and follow up the charge. The makeshift army of drones fills the narrow alley with even more exiting the aircrafts than I can count.

"Um, Rollins?" Ria says in a small voice. "They're getting closer!"

"Rollins?" I call out.

"Hold on," my brother says. He still acts too calm, as he eyes the first row of drones, now only ten or fifteen yards away. "Just a little closer."

The FootSoldiers pick up their pace, lifting their guns in unison.

"Time to go!" Rollins drops his palms to his sides and rockets us into the air. As we gain altitude, the FootSoldiers below squat down on one knee aiming their guns at us.

"We're gonna be target practice for them soon if we don't take cover," I scream out, as the army gets smaller and smaller below. Another idea comes to mind. "Ria! Punch the air!"

Ria swings her free arm around in the shape of an uppercut, slicing through the air. An invisible telekinetic wave glides across the ground below knocking the first dozen Soldiers back a few feet. The force takes out the drones behind them. FootSoldiers fall like dominoes, but the next set of drones behind them starts firing at us.

Rollins maneuvers us through the air as we dodge bullets left and right. Ria releases a strong kick and produces another invisible wave crashing down on our attackers.

We sail around the side of the tall building landing safely down in the street one block over.

"That was too cool," I say, as my feet find the welcome ground underneath.

"They're gonna be on us any second," Rollins says. "We need to find the Metro."

Together, we turn our backs on the gray skyscraper, only to discover another structure even larger. The once-headless statue of Commander Lee stares back at us from the street telling me we are at the north entrance of the Metro. The last time I was standing here, I was arrested.

"Come on," I say, rushing toward a busted-out window on the first floor. "I think I understand what we're supposed to do here now."

CHAPTER 32

BACK AT THE METRO

The entire southeastern side of the building is caved in, but the north entrance is still erect. As we navigate down the labyrinth of halls filled with fallen debris, I tell Ria and Rollins the story about the last time I took cover here and how Kingston saved me from the drone attack.

"He kept talking about this important thing he had to retrieve that a group of NoMads left for him on a computer here," I say, as I lead the way down the dark hallway. Even though the sun was beginning to rise, its rays had not reached the inside of the building yet. "FootSoldiers got him before he could explain, but what if it's the same virus he referred to in the note?"

I spot Rollins nodding his head. "Doc told us about Kingston's visit to him while you were unconscious," my brother begins. "He said Kingston talked about something that could end it all. He didn't know what he meant by it, though."

I nod my head. "I think the key to shutting down Operation Blackbird could have something to do with the virus."

"But NoMads are terrorists." Ria jumps in, confused. "Why would we trust anything they say?"

"Because we have no other choice." I pause and turn toward them. "If you wanna leave now, I understand. I need to see this out for Kingston. If not, then his death will be for nothing." I shudder, again picturing the haunting image of his lifeless body lying on the arena floor.

"I'm not leaving you again," Rollins says, as if rehearsed. "If you say the virus is here, then it's here."

I look over at Ria. I want her to stay, but I'm not sure if I can handle another death on my hands. She didn't ask for any of this...well, none of us did, I guess.

Ria studies the tops of her shoes, as she considers her options. "Ren is being held back at the Compound. I have no choice." Her eyes look up and find mine in the darkness. "And I'm assuming they have August by now, too. I'm not going anywhere either."

A small grin begins to form across my face before I remember what I'm smiling about. "Alright, let's find the computer."

We continue shuffling down the winding hallway, following the trail of fallen ceiling and debris as if they were breadcrumbs leading the way. Nothing looks familiar because the last time I was here, I was forced to crawl through the entire building on my hands and knees in the air ducts while drones fired Tocsins at me from below. Luckily, their path of destruction helps lead us through the hallways that once all appeared identical.

We come across an office whose graffiti-filled door has been blown off its hinges, leaving it lying in scattered chunks. I poke my head in; a single desk sits bare, with a large outline of dust in the center of it.

"I think this is it," I say, entering the small office. I step over the tattered door, then move a broken swivel chair away from the desk.

"So..." Ria says. She stands close behind me. "Where is it?"

"I don't know." I shake my head. "It was right here before." I stretch my hands out, palms down, in the middle of the squared-off, dust border on the desk. "I know we're in the right office. Someone must've taken it."

"You lookin' for somethin'?" A gruff voice echoes out behind us.

All three of us jump.

Rollins draws his knife and holds it out in front of him. "Stay back!"

"Whoa there, son," the homeless-looking man says. "I'm just trying to help you out is all." The man inches closer to us, unafraid of the weapon. His clothes are ragged and bare, making him look like he fought a tornado and lost. He wears an unbuttoned military green shirt that does a poor job of covering him, along with green camouflage pants with as many holes as the shirt. His face is covered in hair and dirt, his curly gray and black locks hanging down in his eyes and off his shoulders.

"Who are you?" I'm standing behind Rollins, raising an arm to hold in front of Ria to protect her.

"The name's Petty." He hawks up phlegm, as he clears his throat. "Whatcha lookin' for?" He studies us like he's a genie about to award us our first wish.

"The computer that was in here?" Ria says in a small, shaky voice.

Rollins keeps the knife out in front of him, attempting to push the man back with threatening motions of the blade.

Petty stops in the doorway, hesitant about entering the small office. "This room has been pretty popular the past few weeks," he begins, before clearing his throat again. "You wouldn't have a smoke by any chance, would ya?"

Rollins shakes his head. "Just get on with it. What do you know about the computer?"

"Since when's anything free in this world?" Petty scratches at a large tangle of matted hair on the side of his head. He scrunches up his nose, as he waits for us to respond.

"We don't have anything," I say, still standing tense behind my brother.

"That knife in your friend's hand will do." A half-smile forms across the homeless man's face.

"You really think..."

"Just give it to him," I say. I exhale, defeated. "We don't have time." I turn my attention back to the man in the doorway. "What do you know?"

Rollins reluctantly hands over the shiny weapon—the second hunting knife that has been taken from him now.

Petty reaches out and accepts the blade. He turns it every which way, waving it around in front of his face to get a better look at it. Once he's satisfied, Petty conceals it in his belt made of rope, after lifting up the back of his shirt. "Well, I saw some Government officials in here a couple of weeks ago after an attack." The man looks up at the ceiling, thinking back. "They boxed everything up. One man said somethin' about going to a Compound or somethin' like that."

The expressions on our faces are identical. We're floored. We came all this way for nothing?

"Did they take any—" I begin, before being cut off by a loudspeaker outside.

"The Metro is surrounded," a mechanical voice booms through the wall behind Petty. I jump in midsentence. "Surrender now and your life will be spared."

Rollins and I look at each other. We knew this was coming. I turn back toward the opening in the door, and Petty is gone. Rollins sticks his head out in the hallway, but the man has disappeared. He punches at the wall just above the powerless light switch.

"Great!" he says, aggravated. "Now we don't even have a weapon."

"Or the virus," I add, piling it on. I exhale loudly.

"At least we know where the computer is now," Ria says with a hint of hope in her small voice.

"Yeah, with no way to get it," my brother says. He scratches at his face. Two-day-old scruff covers his cheeks and neck.

"You have thirty seconds to exit the building," the mechanical voice bellows out through the walls. The image of an army of drones waiting for us outside pops into my head. "Or we will be forced to enter."

"I've got it!" An idea comes rushing at me. "What if we give ourselves up?" I glance back and forth at Ria and Rollins, and watch their immediate negative reactions. I hold my hands out in front of me. "Just hear me out. We need to get back to the Compound somehow, right?"

Both respond with a single bob of the head.

"What if we stage a fake surrender? They'll send us back unknowingly. It's the only way."

"And lock us up," Ria adds, like it's the dumbest plan she's ever heard.

"Or worse." Rollins echoes her tone. "If they even take us back at all, they'll throw us in the re-education dorms. Re-Ed is sick. It's like a psych ward. You don't wanna end up there."

"Twenty seconds."

"Then tell them that I kidnapped the two of you." My panicky eyes shoot back and forth between the two of them. "I made you both do all of this. I'll go in Re-Ed. Tell them it was all my idea."

Rollins immediately shakes his head. "Not a chance. I'm your older brother. I'll take the fall."

"Fifteen seconds."

"Rollins," I say, as I turn to face him, "you can't protect me forever. Let me do this. Please."

I watch my brother's eyes weigh the decision. He exhales to tell me he still doesn't approve, but he knows we don't have the time to argue. "Fine. What do you want us to do?"

CHAPTER 33

SURRENDER

A metal canister crashes through a still partially intact window across the hall. The office begins to fill with gray smoke, which then seeps out into the hallway and into the office where we are huddled together.

"Cover your mouth," Rollins says flatly. "That smoke can be anything. Stay low and let's move."

We rush back down the hallway in the same direction we just came from and follow the trail of debris back to the north entrance.

"You two run out first," I say. A plan forms in my head. "Tell them you escaped." I give a deep cough, my throat irritated by the cloud of smoke winding down the hall.

Rollins grits his teeth, still not accepting the idea of me taking all of the blame. He realizes we can't all be locked up in Re-Ed—that someone will have to be free to search for the computer, so he goes along with it.

"What if they shoot you?" Ria looks up at me like the idea hasn't crossed my mind a hundred times since coming up with the plan. Her breathing rate has increased and her chest heaves up and down in short bursts.

"It's the chance I have to take," I say, as I reach out for her. "There's no other way back."

Ria grabs my hands, and I pull her to my chest. She raises herself up a few inches, standing on her tiptoes. Our lips meet and share what could be our last kiss. I pull back to release her, but she holds me in for a few more seconds before ending the kiss. For a very brief moment, everything else seems to fall by the wayside. The only thing that is important is the two of us—not the army of drones outside or the missing computer…us.

I lick the tip of my upper lip, wishing we'd met under different circumstances. No girl has ever expressed even the slightest bit of interest in me and now, when one finally does, I'm a wanted fugitive by the Government's Army.

"Just remember," I remind them again, "it was all my idea."

I release my grip from Ria's hands and allow the two of them to run out of the building before I can change my mind. They exit through the same busted-out window we came in from earlier. Their hands are already raised over their heads, eyes staring down at the pavement before them.

"Get down on your knees," the same booming voice orders through the speakers. "Place your hands on top of your head."

A group of six human Tele soldiers, all dressed in black and wearing the circular Operation Blackbird patch on their sleeves, rush toward the entrance where my brother and Ria kneel, frozen on the ground. Handcuffs are slapped across their wrists before forcing them to their feet. Steel helmets are placed over both of their heads, preventing them from performing any telekinetic stunts to escape. I watch from inside the building as they are rushed off the road and out of sight.

"Nicholas McCready, we have the entire building surrounded. Surrender now or we will be forced to enter. The other Teles have been captured."

I mimic Rollins and Ria, as I exit the Metro with my hands to the sky, eyes glued to the road in front of me. "I give up," I shout. "It was all me!"

I'm ordered to get down on my knees before glancing up. Two Tele soldiers rush toward me, while a large group of drones hold their guns on me just in case I get the idea to run. Off to the side, behind the army of FootSoldiers, the original six soldiers who came out to handcuff Rollins and Ria are patting their new prisoners down for weapons. One soldier, who wears a malicious smirk across his face, pats Ria across her chest.

"Look at this one," the soldier says, with a laugh, to the boy next to him, who has his gun drawn. He holds it inches away from the back of Ria's head. "They're not usually this cute...or easy!"

I furrow my brows, my mouth gaping open. "Hey!" I yell out in their direction. "Get off her!" In all of the commotion surrounding us, my threat is lost in the early morning breeze. I push myself halfway up, only to be struck in the ribs with the butt end of a gun. I hear a loud crack. I keel over on my side, my ribs crying out in unbelievable pain.

"Stay down and shut up," a raucous voice orders me. The soldier spits down on the concrete inches away from my face. My hands are cuffed behind my back, allowing the soldier standing over me to kick me in my already hurt ribs.

I roll around on my side in pain, wincing, as I attempt to suck in some air to choke out a yell. "Get off..." I scream out between breaths, as a tinted helmet is placed over my face blacking out my visual surroundings.

Whoop, Whoop, Whoop, Whoop...

I sense an engine close by starting up, followed by something that sounds like it's slapping at the air.

I'm lifted off the ground by two soldiers, each man hooking an arm through mine. They drag me forward toward the loud, slapping air sound. My ribs feel like they're on fire.

"Keep your head down, McCready. We wouldn't want you to lose it before you return home." The two soldiers cackle.

The whooping sound increases, which tells me I'm being put into a helicopter. The soldiers strap me to a seat, locking me in for the ride. I try turning my head in both directions, but I'm paralyzed. A mirrored image of my face flashes back at me through my visor.

The plan worked. We're heading back to the Compound.

I just hope Ria and Rollins are along for the ride, too.

CHAPTER 34

RE-ED

Two clicks ring out, followed by a strong suction sound. The helmet is pulled from my face, and right away my eyes squint into the bright shining light cascading down from overhead. Everything in Re-Ed is pink—the walls, my clothes, the floor, the bed—even the toilet in the corner. The place reminds me of the medicine my mom used to give me when I was younger whenever I had an upset stomach.

One Tele soldier dressed in black stands armed in the entrance of my open cell. His partner unlocks my handcuffs from behind, freeing my hands.

I massage my wrists as I try to work out a kink in both hands.

"What are they gonna do to me?" I question the soldier closest to me named Isbell, but he doesn't say a word. "Where are the two Teles they brought in with me?"

"You don't worry about them," the soldier standing in front of the door responds for his partner. "You best just worry about yourself."

The two soldiers exit the cell and lock the barred door behind them. Someone in another cell farther down the hall whimpers aloud to himself.

"Hey, you okay?" I shout, only to cause a sharp shooting pain to rifle through my sore ribs. I grimace, holding my side with both hands. Someone wrapped up my torso in the helicopter while making our short trip back to the Compound. I can only imagine what my ribs look like underneath.

The same person lets out another yelp followed by sniffles. Whoever's down there is in pretty bad shape. I close my eyes and sit on the single cot in my cell, which makes the paper-thin mattress lift up on either side of me. Even the slightest body movement makes me want to cry out in pain.

I let out a muffled groan when I try to raise my arms over my head to take off the pink shirt. I come to the conclusion that it's useless. I lift the edge of my shirt before slowly unwrapping the gauze from around my midsection. A large purple bruise is visible, covering the majority of my injured side. I sit up straight as I attempt to let out a deep breath. Even breathing hurts.

Another loud moan comes from down the hall, but it seems closer than before. Then I hear someone mumbling.

"Can't take it anymore," the voice mutters to himself. "Just can't take it."

My eyes spin around the room landing on a small AC vent in the lower corner in front of my cot. I gingerly lie the top half of my body down, carefully sprawled out across the cot so my head is closer to the vent. If I can hear him, then he should be able to hear me.

"Are...you...there?" I say, forcing out the question between spurts of pain.

The moaning stops.

"Down here in the vent," I somehow manage to squeeze out all in one breath. Lying on my side is only making it worse, so I push myself back up, sliding my back up against the wall behind me. "How long have you been here?"

"Not sure," the deep voice answers back through the vent. "Maybe a few weeks? Months?"

"What did you do?" I turn my mouth down toward the vent a little more.

"Lee sent me here after our meeting," the toneless voice answers. "After I tried to kill him."

The sound of stomping boots interrupts our brief conversation. The same two Tele soldiers from earlier appear outside the bars. I look up just as both of them glance over.

The soldier closest to my cell's door halts and places a hand between the bars. "No talking in Re-Ed!"

I nod, forcing them to keep moving.

As soon as they pass, I lean my head back down toward the vent.

"What's your name?"

No answer.

"Again?" The voice sounds muffled again, as if its owner has moved away from the vent.

"On your feet, recruit. You know the procedure."

Seconds later, I hear the distant cell door click shut, followed by a set of three footsteps marching in my direction. As the trio passes, only the recruit in the center looks over in my direction. He's much bigger than his two guards, in height and in muscle, but his hands are cuffed behind his back, along with steel shackles around his feet. His face is unmasked, allowing him to turn his head toward my cell.

August!

CHAPTER 35

MEETING WITH LEE

The absent look on August's face turns to disbelief as our eyes lock in passing. His mouth opens to question, but I shake my head at him with a subtle jerk forcing him to close it. Soldier Isbell glances over at me expressionless as they pass my cell. The echoing sound of their footsteps continues until they exit the hallway.

August has been here the whole time?

I think back to the day I followed him in the woods—the day I was captured and brought here. What was he doing out there? It doesn't matter now. I'm stuck in here with fractured ribs, not knowing what's going on with the missing computer and virus...or with Ria and Rollins.

And what did that kiss mean? Was she only thanking me for taking the fall?

My drifting eyes focus on the center of the hot pink wall facing me. I roll my shoulders back in an effort to find a halfway comfortable position.

"Your turn, recruit."

I glance up to discover the same two Tele soldiers standing on the other side of the bars. I didn't even hear them approach the cell.

"Commander Lee requests a word with you," Isbell says in a somewhat friendly tone, as he unlocks the steel door. The sliding door rattles open. "Stand up and place both of your hands behind your back."

"My ribs are broken," I cry out. "I'm not going anywhere!" I pout and look down at the ground, trying to buy some time. I can't see Lee now. I haven't found Rollins or Ria yet. I don't even know the plan.

The soldier who was standing guard at the door earlier enters alone. He leaves his partner on the other side. The name Morrison is sewn above his shirt pocket.

"You have five seconds to get up off that bed." Morrison hovers over me. His voice is calm, but his facial expression tells me otherwise. He massages the trigger with his index finger. A bright red light shoots out of the back of his neck, bouncing off the wall across from the cell.

"I'm not going anywhere until I see a doctor." I glue my eyes to the pink floor between my legs.

The Tele soldier reaches out, grabs me with one hand under the shoulder and jerks me up onto my feet. I let out a loud groan, sinking back down to the floor.

"Get up, McCready!" he barks out at me. He straps his gun around his neck and pulls it to the side. Keeping his eyes on me, he draws a long thin bar from around his waist, yanking out the extension piece on the end. "We can do this the easy way or the hard way." He flips a switch and the weapon begins to buzz, the tip turning fiery red. He pulls back his hand and holds the glowing baton behind his head, ready to strike me with it.

"Okay, okay," I say exhaling. I push myself up under my own power. There's only so much I can take. Our eyes meet as I turn toward him, straightening my back. "I'm up," I answer, even as I grit my teeth.

Morrison clicks off the baton and straps it back on his belt.

We exit the cell, only to quickly enter an elevator. I sense the elevator moving down several floors, but it's moving so fast I cannot be sure.

The doors open, and I look up only to see a dark visor rapidly pulled over my eyes. The protective helmet is fastened under my chin locking out all of my senses but one, so I listen.

The sound of three pairs of boots echoes out in unison, the pattern clicking and clacking, bouncing off the nearby walls. Walls that appear so close, it sounds like I could reach out and touch them if I stood in the middle, and, of course, if my hands were free.

The guard to my right coughs, but we continue without pause

before coming to a sudden jerked stop.

After a few seconds, a loud, single beep rings out, forcing us to move again.

Almost immediately, we come to another jerking stop.

"We're here to see Commander Lee, sir," Morrison announces to someone before us. "We have Recruit Nicholas McCready from Re-Ed."

Without verbal confirmation, we move forward, both Tele soldiers digging back in under my shoulders as they get a better grip on me. I push a groan back down my throat.

We walk a few steps and stop before I'm shoved into a chair.

"Remove the helmet," a deep booming voice commands, sending the Tele soldier on my right to fumble nervously at the head device. He unlatches it from underneath my chin. A suction sound echoes as the headgear rises up.

I look across the desk from where I'm sitting and a tan-skinned man in a black suit stares back at me with a grimace. He's in shape, filling the suit out. His white shirt collar is open. His hair is combed over, parted to the side with not a single strand out of place. The man looks like a millionaire, not a ruthless military commander.

"Hello, Nicholas. Welcome back."

CHAPTER 36

PUNISHMENT

Commander Lee looks different. He has gone through numerous physical changes since the last time he went public—after the Uprising—but I can see it in his intense eyes that it's him. There are some things you cannot alter. It's him. It's definitely him. He's the reason why I'm here. Why Rollins and Ria are here.

"Do you remember me, Nicholas?"

I stare back at him, refusing to speak. The soldier standing to my right draws back his elbow and launches it into my sore ribs. I double over, burying my face in my stomach.

"The commander asked you a question," Morrison spits out, leaning over me.

"That's okay," Lee says, relaxed. He holds up a hand to inform the soldier that the force wasn't necessary. "He'll talk after I have a few words with him. I'm sure of it."

I roll my eyes and bite down on the edge of my bottom lip. I look around the large office, focusing on the larger-than-life-size mural of Commander Lee painted on the wall behind his desk. It stretches from floor to the ceiling, extending out in both directions with a desert background behind him. Lee's dressed in his flawlessly pressed military uniform with various metals and stripes covering his shirt. His hand rests on top of his pistol still holstered around his waist, while his other hand hangs to the side. His menacing eyes stare forward, locking onto mine.

"You know you caused us a quite a bit of trouble and resources returning you to the Compound, Nicholas. You should be grateful for our actions." Lee releases a snort under his breath, amusing himself. "We could have simply left you in Sol to be arrested. Would you have preferred that?"

"For being a Tele?" I spit out. My petulant eyes find the commander's.

The smirk doesn't leave his face, but his eyes grow smaller. Lee glances to the side for a few seconds before leaning forward. I sense the air leave the room.

"Have you figured out what we're doing here?" He pauses, as he waits for a response. "People like you who have these special gifts inside them have to be trained how to use them; to fight the good fight. There's a group of terrorists living within our own country who I'm sure you're aware of." His eyes look me up and down, assessing me. "Nicholas, the NoMads want nothing more than to destroy this great country of ours. Do you wish to see that happen?"

His condescending questions make my blood boil.

Morrison pulls back his elbow again, threatening me to answer the commander.

I feel my head jerk to the side, even though I didn't tell it to.

"That's what I thought. You're special, you know, Nicholas McCready." The way my name rolls off his tongue sounds creepier than the staring mural over the commander's back looks. "We wouldn't have spent so much effort and resources to retrieve you if you weren't needed here. Was it really that much better in Sol?"

I inch forward in my seat, as I adjust my position. "At least there I wasn't locked up in a pink cage, not knowing what's going to happen to me—my mind being altered and controlled like some kind of a drone." I sniffle and keep my eyes locked on Lee, refusing to be intimidated.

"Oh yes, the re-education dorms," he says, with a growing smile on his face. "We simply could not trust you in the regular dorms. Not yet, anyway. You have to prove yourself first. You see, Operation Blackbird is much bigger than me or you. When the Government made it illegal to perform a telekinetic act in public, we had to figure out what to do with all of the Teles. The prisons were already well over capacity, so we couldn't lock all of you up. We had to find something useful for the Teles to do, a way for them to use their power for the good of the country. So I created Operation

Blackbird: a super-army of sorts, who, with the proper training, will eliminate the world's terrorists, starting in our own country. It had to be done, Nicholas. It's the only way. Think of it kind of like a draft, but for Teles."

"There are other ways," I say, holding back the endless list of curse words I want to shout out at the top of my lungs. "This isn't right!"

"Don't you think for a second you're the first Tele to sit across from me spouting that nonsense." Commander Lee shifts in his chair, catching the light across his face. Under his eye, a thin red scar runs down his cheek to just above his jaw line...a scar that wasn't there the last time we spoke via the Prompter. "You have two options here is how I see it: learn to use your abilities to the fullest and join the Government's Army or spend the rest of your days in Re-Ed. The choice is yours. This doesn't stop in Sol. There are Compounds all over the east coast, commanders in each of the sectors recruiting more and more Teles each day, building stronger armies than this country has ever seen." His hands rise up at his sides, as if he's showing me something magical around him.

The feeling of deflation enters my body. I have always wondered what it might look like outside of Sol, but I never imagined it full of Teles running around in fear of being arrested and hauled off to a place like this.

"Whatever you decide, you still have to be punished." The tone in Lee's voice changes gravely. "Last time, I was too easy on you." The corner of his mouth curls up making him appear even more intimidating. "Since you have arrived, you've tested off the charts. You need a challenge in the arena—someone who will truly test your abilities to determine how powerful you really are."

The commander nods his head in the direction of the two soldiers standing on either side of me. They place their heavy hands on my shoulder blades, digging in for a likely struggle.

"Someone you know very well." He leans forward in his large leather chair a little more, and his fresh red scar almost glows in the light.

He's already had me in the arena with Ria. Which other recruit could be worse—August?

Then, as soon as he opens his mouth, it hits me...

"Your next battle in the arena will be against your older brother,

Rollins."

CHAPTER 37

ROOT

A full three days have passed since my meeting with Lee. My ribs have healed after a visit to the on-base Healer right after the meeting. I'm able to move around pain-free now, but I'm still confined to my tiny Re-Ed cell. The headaches have started to recede, but an annoying itch still bothers me on the back of the neck—both telling side effects of a recent re-Wash I knew was coming.

"Lunch-time," a female's voice calls out.

That's a first. Other than Ria, I have yet to see another female Tele since coming here. The image of Ria's face pops in my head. In just three days, I've grown to miss her so much—her feathery pink bangs that seem never to want to stay in place; her smile that curls up in just in the corner of her mouth; her gentle touch she knows I find reassuring. Could it really be her?

I jump up off my cot and latch onto the bars in front of me.

An olive-skinned girl with small, narrow eyes, possibly fifteen or sixteen years old, creeps up to the door towing a small food cart behind her. She has on the recruit's standard uniform, dressed all in white from head to toe. Her straight dark hair is pulled back in a ponytail. She looks pure. The girl turns away to unlatch the food cart. She pulls a fresh tray off an inside middle shelf. The tattoo of the blackbird is embedded into her skin halfway hidden underneath her long hair telling me she's currently under her own power since the tattoo isn't glowing red.

"Nicholas?" she questions, wide-eyed, as she holds onto the tray of food with both hands.

I nod and study her face.

"I'm Root. I work in the kitchen with your friend Ria." She speaks good English, but with an unusual accent.

I light up, tightening my grip around the steel bars. "Is she okay?" I shout.

She nods her head, assuring me. She slides the food tray through the open slot in the door. "She's okay. She told me to give you a message: she has located the virus and has passed it on to a friend in the control room. He will activate it during your next battle."

A feeling of relief rushes over me before I go over the plan in my head. "Wait, who is it? Someone we can trust?"

Root shakes her head. "That's all she told me, Nicholas. I'm sorry, but I have to go." There is sudden a hint of fear in her voice. "I don't want to get in trouble."

"What about my brother, Rollins?" I question further, pulling my face even closer to the bars. "What happened to him? Where are they keeping him?"

Root opens her mouth to answer, but is cut off.

"Is there a problem here, recruit?" Bootsteps reverberate off the shiny floor heading this way. "There's no talking in Re-Ed!"

Root turns her head in the direction of the approaching footsteps. "No problem at all." Her voice cracks. "Just delivering the lunch trays." She turns her attention back to me, as she covers the corner of her mouth. "I'll be back as soon as I can," she mumbles.

A Tele soldier whom I've never seen before this morning trudges up to the food cart. He's older, maybe seventeen or eighteen years old with short blond hair and a nose that appears to have been broken many times throughout his short life. A thin red bar of light shoots out the back of his neck reflecting off the pink wall behind it. He sticks his index finger into the center of the chocolate pudding on my tray, stirring it around before popping the chocolate-covered finger between his lips. He makes a kissing sound, pulling it free from his mouth. "Leave the food and move on. Everyone in Re-Ed is here for a reason."

Root steals another quick glance back at me before complying with her orders. She nods before positioning herself behind the food cart, forced to continue down the line. The wheels on the cart begin to squeak, but quickly fade the farther she moves down the hall.

The soldier turns to leave as I pull the tray inward and turn up my nose. I still haven't gotten used to the food. I sit on my cot and place the tray over my knees. I glance down at the silent AC vent in the corner of the room for the hundredth time in the past three days. August never returned to his cell after being hauled off to the arena for a battle. Either something serious happened, or they're keeping him elsewhere now. Did someone hear us talking?

I pick up my spork and push a solid, cold piece of meat around the center of the plate.

"Looks like you're getting the call in the morning," the same broken-nosed soldier says. He returns to my cell. "You best eat up. You'll need your strength in the arena tomorrow." He cackles loudly, before turning back in the direction he just came from.

CHAPTER 38

BLACKOUT

At dawn, or at least what feels like dawn in here, I find myself pacing my cell as I wait for someone to come and get me. My cell door rattles open, forcing me to sit on the cot. A single FootSoldier drone stands at attention in the doorway. I guess they didn't trust a Tele soldier to escort me after what happened last time with Rollins.

"On your feet, recruit," the robotic voice booms. Its red sadistic eyes scan the entire length of my cot. Within seconds it has my identity, history, body temperature, blood pressure, heart rate— nothing short of a full body probe.

I rub at my swollen eyes before pushing myself up. I get dressed, huddled in the corner, the drone refusing to give me any form of privacy.

I'm handcuffed again, along with having a protective helmet shoved down over my face. My drooping eyes reflect back against the mirror-like visor. My escort latches onto my arm, pulling me down the hall and into the elevator, as I drag my feet for the first few steps.

I really wish I knew more of the plan. A picture of Rollins pops in my head. Will the virus be activated before either of us even has to enter the arena? What if Ria's friend fails? Will I really have to fight my own brother?

What if I fail?

The drone leads me down the staircase and halts, without warning, on the bottom level in front of the red door that I can't see, but I know is there. I hear the usual muffled voices shouting out on the other side, only to be interrupted by a single loud beep, informing us to enter.

I breathe in deeply; my heart rate increases. The FootSoldier standing in front of me frees my hands before unlatching the headgear. The red door slides open before me; the surrounding audience drowned out by the suction noise I always hear as the helmet is pulled free from my head. A strong shove from behind pushes me out onto the arena floor.

I stumble to the ground, falling on my hands and knees.

Instantly, the crowd turns on me, pushing me back with their hatred and mockery. I scramble back up against the red door as it comes down. The exit is now sealed off.

I force myself to stand and press my hands up against the middle of the door behind me, peering across the floor. The center of the arena floor is lit up, but this time all of the surrounding areas are stained black—including the stands. The once transparent wall is now curtained black. I take a couple steps out, walking toward the dark barrier. A black metallic mirror flashes back an image of a stranger. My bulging gut is gone from around my midsection and my face has thinned. My hair is cut short, but I've started growing facial hair in faint patches along my cheeks and chin. How long have I been here?

I straighten my back, as I roll my shoulders. I can still hear the crowd shouting through the opaque wall, so I know they're there. They must be able to see me, even though they're hidden.

In the reflection before me, I watch the door slide open from across the floor. No introduction. No opponent's music. The door rises, a large shadow immediately casts out. A few seconds later, Rollins is shoved forward onto the ground by a FootSoldier, mimicking my entrance. Even though he has given a year of his life to these people, to this place, they still treat him like an unwanted animal.

My brother defensively pushes himself off the ground, his eyes finding me across the way.

Is he under Lee's control?

Am I?

Has the battle even begun?

Rollins's eyes look tired and confused. Like me, he has probably been up most of the night. His head turns, his eyes flying around the arena. He takes a step forward in my direction, until a loud, heavy roar rumbles out from across the way and he freezes in place.

A hidden door to my right, normally blocked by various makeshift arena weapons, has come to life, rising into the ceiling. A long dark shadow pauses before moving across the floor. The crowd to my back cheers even louder, as if they're in on the secret of who it is.

My eyes narrow as they peer across the distance. The shadow soon develops into a figure as Kingston steps out from the doorframe. His eyes focus on Rollins before finding me in the opposite corner of the arena. The burn hole on his face has healed, leaving no visible trace of the acid.

How is he alive?

By now nothing here should shock me anymore. I guess a Healer can cure a dead person, too. Good to know.

Kingston takes another step or two into the illuminated section of the large room before halting. A single red beam rockets out the back of his neck and bounces off the now closed door to his rear. A deadpan look covers his face. He's no longer looking at me, but staring across the floor, eying nothing in particular, as if waiting on something or someone.

The crowd begins to beat on the wall behind me in unison. The pounding echoes louder and louder, filling the arena, absorbing any confidence I might still hold that our plan will work.

I stare across the floor, my waiting eyes questioning Rollins. *What now?*

Another rumble follows, out to my left. A fourth door opens in the final corner of the arena. Out comes another long, dark shadow filling a large portion of the lit floor in the center. August steps out, the back of his neck matching Kingston's, telling me they're both under Lee's control. Both of his eyes have a black ring around them; his nose is off-centered.

"Ladies and gentleman," a voice begins over the loudspeaker, subduing the audience. "We have a special treat for you today with a four-man battle royale!"

It takes me a second, but I identify Lee over the loudspeakers. His voice seems to hypnotize the crowd, each spectator hanging on his every word.

"The rules have not changed, other than throwing a couple of extra bodies into the mix." I can sense his trademark malicious smile forming as he talks. "Like usual, we can only have one victor. The last person standing will be declared the winner and will advance into the officers' program."

As Lee finishes his sentence, I spy Kingston's head flip to the side, his eyes locking onto Rollins from across the way. He lifts out his hand and fires a metal folding chair off in my brother's direction. Rollins ducks in time and watches the chair ricochet off the solid coal-black wall over his shoulder.

With all my attention focused on Kingston and Rollins battling it out across the room, I ignore the charging rhino disguised in the form of August, bull-rushing low from the opposite corner. I turn my head just as he tackles me head on across the chest, sending us both sliding across the floor. The back of my head strikes the wall behind me with a thud.

The crowd lets out an, "Ewww…" as my skull makes impact with the solid barrier.

"Did I fail to mention that the battle has begun?" Lee comes back sounding condescending over the loudspeaker, proud that at least one of his attacks was successful.

The crowd roars, punctuating the commander's statement with an exclamation point.

I attempt to push August off me, shoving his face away as his enormous right hand connects with the side of my head. His fist feels like it punches through my eardrum, sending the inside of my head into mass confusion. My vision becomes blurry as I try to prop myself up against the wall behind me, kicking and pushing August away. I misjudge the distance and stumble over to the side. I collapse onto the cold ground.

August stands and turns around. His eyes search for something to throw at me. He lifts his hand and levitates an old filing cabinet from the nearest corner. The metal box hovers a few feet off the ground, strangely refusing to leave its home corner. August appears to struggle with the weight of the cabinet or the ability to eject it. The rectangular box wobbles in the air, before it slowly sinks back down to the ground before rising again.

Is he fighting the control over his mind? Is that even possible?

Taking full advantage of the hiccup, I get my bearings and

gingerly push myself up. I turn my head around in time to spot the weightless filing cabinet sailing across the room toward me. I twist out of the way at the last second, but the bottom edge of the cabinet strikes my shoulder and the side of my already pounding face.

The force knocks me back down and I land face first on the ground. I feel like I was run over by a bulldozer.

I shake my head in an attempt to find some clarity, while at the same time searching for August across the floor. I see everything double…triple.

No August.

I spin around, promptly spotting Kingston and Rollins still battling it out on the opposite end of the arena. They're both somewhat blurred and seem really far away, but it looks like Rollins is winning the fight. The crowd continues to yell to my rear, forcing me to swing back around. All of a sudden, the intensity all around me seems to have increased. Sweat pours down my face; my head's swimming.

I spot August off to the side, crouched down on one knee. He holds his forehead.

A loud pop goes off in my head that causes me to tense up. Everything is blurry again and moving in slow motion. Pushing everything around me away, I swipe my hand across my face. I feel comatose inside as trails of all the different colors of the rainbow shoot out of my arm.

My body turns toward the corner of the room where August remains down on one knee. I lock onto my target.

The words, *Kill August* erupt in my head like a volcano.

And then it repeats itself over and over again, until I only have one thought in my head.

I must kill August.

CHAPTER 39

ACTIVATED

My head rotates, as I search for a weapon to use.

The dented filing cabinet lies close by on its side, jammed up against the stained black wall behind me. Mysterious, translucent waves of steam dance off the top of the rectangular box, evaporating a few inches above it in thin air.

My arm ascends before me, leveling out on its own. The filing cabinet rises and levitates to my side like an obedient pet waiting to play fetch. With a quick flip of the wrist, I fling the metal box away and strike a confused, kneeling August across the top of his broad back.

August lets out a guttural roar, his body tensing up on impact. He collapses forward, the side of his face burying itself into the arena floor.

He's out cold.

Satisfied, I gradually turn my head toward the opposite end of the arena. A hard-fought battle is going on between two figures in the distance. I force my eyes to focus on the faces of the fighters, but they remain blurred. I take a few steps forward before a strong, commanding voice enters my brain forcing me to halt.

Kill August. Kill everyone. You are the one, true champion.

My heartbeat increases and matches my breathing. Adrenalin pumps wildly through my veins. An animal instinct runs through me, and, like a vampire, my body craves fresh blood.

Somewhere deep down, though, something inside pushes me to

fight the urge. This isn't right.

I shake my head and grunt. I release a loud groan, as I tilt head back like a wolf, determined to take back control over my own body. My lips attempt to form the word No, only to feel a sharp bolt of pain erupting up from the back of my neck before spilling out into my head.

I bend over feeling nauseated, dizzy.

Sweat rains down from my forehead. I rest my hands on my knees. My legs feel unbalanced like they're about to give out underneath me. A soft voice mumbles something in my head, but I can't make it out.

An object in the shape of a sphere rolls up and ricochets off the edge of my shoe. My eyes spot a lead pipe about the length of my arm rolling a few inches away from my foot before coming to a stop.

I watch my hand reach for the metal rod and lift it in the air. An image of three figures lying motionless on the arena floor burns in my mind. All three bodies are lined up next to each other, each covered by a single white sheet. A pipe, tipped in dark red blood, rests close by.

A smile forms across my face.

As I pull back my wrist, I feel a powerful force plow into my side that sends us both across the floor in a ball. A huge fist makes contact under my chin before another finds my left eye.

August is yelling something. He grabs and shakes me by my shirt, but his voice is muffled, as if he has a rag stuffed in his mouth.

I swipe my arm across his body and smack August in the nose, giving me enough time to whip up my palm.

August rockets off me just as another loud pop echoes throughout my head, followed by another excruciating pain bubbling up in the base of my neck. My eyes bug out and my body levitates off the ground about an inch, before collapsing back down.

Everything freezes.

The black sheet that once blanketed the entire inside of the arena falls like curtains, opening up the building around us. No longer is the invisible barrier black, but transparent again. The unusually subdued audience is revealed.

A semi-automatic gun goes off behind me, spraying the see-through wall with bullets. Multiple small cracks erupt in each of the places the ammo struck above me, giving way to larger fissures before the translucent material shatters. I crane my head and spot Logan wresting a Tele soldier to the ground. He rips away the older teen's gun.

Another gun fires off a couple of rounds on the opposite side of the arena. Frightened, wide-eyed recruits and Tele soldiers begin pouring out of the stands. They jump down onto the floor. Both groups seem equally confused on what to do.

August comes to and lifts himself up, just in time to get out of the way of a stampede of recruits running away from a determined Tele soldier. He wipes a trail of blood off his forehead before something catches his eye and he points off to the side.

"Nic!" he shouts out. "Get…"

The same Tele soldier rushes up behind him. He smashes the butt-end of the gun across the back of August's skull. I watch in shock as his eyes roll to the back of his head, his legs giving out underneath him.

Wanting to help, my body flinches just enough to get the soldier's attention. His legs widen into a stance; one of his boots kicks August in the side of the head before finding me about ten or fifteen yards away.

"Freeze," the soldier calls out. He forces me to throw my hands up. He shoves his gun forward. "You are still under arrest!" The Tele soldier takes a small step forward, sidestepping around the bulk of August's body on the ground. He looks back up at me with a smirk, just as the barrel side of a metal baseball bat comes down across the back of his skull. The Tele soldier slumps to the side.

Rollins stands over him. He uses the bat to point off in the same direction as August.

The fog has lifted from the inside of my head. On the far side of the arena, Commander Lee is standing over someone in the control room angrily yelling down at them. Like the rest of the building, the tinted windows are gone. The small room and its occupants are exposed for the first time.

"I'll stay here and get everyone together," Rollins shouts out to me. A large gash has opened across the top of his shaved head. Blood runs down over his eyes and the side of his face. "You go after Lee. We'll meet in the hangar!"

I nod. "I'm not leaving without you and Ria!"

My brother shakes his head before evading an incoming attack by a Tele soldier. Rollins flips the attacker over his shoulder and onto the ground, then his hand slices through the air, palm up. An invisible force strikes the helmetless soldier in his only uncovered spot. It sends the boy flying off into the opposite corner of the room.

I dash across the arena toward the control room, dodging countless Tele soldiers arresting loose recruits running around wild and confused.

As I reach for the door handle, I feel a heavy hand thump down on my shoulder and pull me back. I flip my forearm up and smack a Tele soldier in the bridge of his nose. He stumbles back, losing his footing. His gun clinks to the ground, as it slides away from him.

I turn back toward the door. My eyes instantly connect with someone inside the control room—Lee. He reaches for something down by his feet, his other hand clutching a pistol inches in front of his face.

I raise my hand pulling the knob off and kick the door open. Bullets spray the backside of the heavy door as I slam it shut. My eyes dart around the control room. The lights are down low with only a few lamps on. Television monitors in all different sizes cover the walls each with an occupied chair facing it. Ren, sitting in one of the seats on the far side of the room, turns to face me.

"Where's Lee?" I scream out.

Multiple scared, confused faces stare back at me, all refusing to talk.

My eyes land back on Ren again. He points across the room toward a dark hallway.

"And he has Ria."

CHAPTER 40

COUNTDOWN

I start for the hallway, when I hear a series of loud beeps over the Compound's loudspeaker—a warning of something to come. Across the room, television monitors flip to an image of a woman's face staring forward, as if she isn't aware she's live on camera. She has a long, thin face with shoulder-length gray and black hair, parted down the middle. A small, fading scar runs vertically between her eyes just above her nose. She's dressed in old fashioned, conservative clothes. The top button is fastened on her frilly white blouse and it's covered by a navy blue sweater buttoned halfway up. The top tip of a blue tattoo sneaks out of the collar of her blouse.

The woman shifts forward, lifting her eyes as if given the cue to begin her speech. She clears her throat.

"The Government has been lying to you since you were born," she begins, talking in a slow monotone, as if she's just learned how to speak English. "Commander Lee is a coward and war criminal who must pay for his actions, as do all of you." The woman clears her throat again. She looks downward, with a grave expression. "Now that the barriers are down, your Compound will be exterminated by NoMad forces, ending the evil and corruption that has gone on for entirely too long there. We wish there was another way, but there is not. We do all of this in the name of our people. For our once-great country. Godspeed."

The woman's eyes close, signaling the monitors to go dark. The entire control room erupts into a mass panic. Chatter turns into a shouting match, each person blaming another for their current situation. I peer out onto the arena floor. Groups of recruits and Tele soldiers have formed, presumably discussing what they all just heard.

A red screen counting down from thirty minutes replaces the dark monitors. The new image produces a sinister red glow around the room. The ticking sound of a clock rings out over the speakers.

Tick, tock, tick, tock, tick...

"Find August," I yell over to Ren. "I'm gonna get Ria!"

I exit the control room and race down the dark hallway, passing large groups of armed Tele soldiers rushing in the opposite direction. The hallway splits off into two directions, and intuition pushes me to the right, the less active path of the two.

I turn the corner to find a set of closing elevator doors. As the edges of the two doors are becoming one, I raise my palm in midstride and widen the crevice into a bigger opening. I squeeze in before the doors can close behind me. The empty elevator rises on its own, and it builds up speed.

I lean back and hold onto the rail. The elevator climbs floor after floor before jerking to a stop. A single bell rings out before the doors in front of me open.

The sound of the artificial clock counting down continues its warning. It ominously echoes out overhead.

I step out onto the marble flooring. Bright, white lights illuminate a path down the hallway. I turn my head, unsure of which direction to go until I hear a girl's voice cry out from the far end of the hall.

"Ahhhh, get away from me! You're crazy!"

Ria.

I rush off in the direction of the scream, charging down the hallway before I skid to a halt at the lone door in the hall. It's cracked open, light and voices spilling out. Lee is behind his desk waving a gun around. His eyes search for something on his desk.

"If it wasn't for your friends, you wouldn't be in this mess, would you?" Lee doesn't look up, but I know who he's talking to.

I creep to the side and peer closer into the cracked doorway, searching for Ria. Huddled into the corner, she sits in a ball. Her back is pushed as far up against the corner of the room as possible, her knees pulled up to her chin. Her matted hair falls down across her face, the tips wet from her tears. She lets out a series of sniffles

179

while holding a hand over her eye.

"Oh, will you shut it?" Lee's annoyed voice shouts. He glances over into the corner. "I need to keep you alive a little longer; a little insurance just in case any of your friends get the wrong idea." Lee glances back down, continuing his search through the papers and folders on his desk. He pulls out a tablet and types something into the keyboard. "When the attack comes, you won't even feel it. First your organs will shut down, then your body will liquefy, turning you into a puddle of nothing."

Tick, tock, tick, tock, tick...

My eyes widen. I can't let that happen. I barrel into the office and slam the door against the wall.

Startled, Lee looks up, as I lift my palm. He's faster than me, though.

He fires his gun, hitting me in the shoulder. My body flies backward and I land on my back with a thud. A loud, piercing bell rings out in my head, the noise blurring my vision.

At first, I don't feel a thing. I can hear my heartbeat thumping in my ears. I think he's missed until I look over at my arm and there's a small red hole filling with blood. I let out a moan as I try to lift myself up, only to increase the pain. My shoulder burns like it's on fire.

As if he's in no hurry, Lee takes his time walking around from the other side of his desk. The frightened, surprised look he was wearing when I rushed into his office is now gone, replaced with his infamous scowl.

"You think you're so smart, McCready? You can't beat me." He bends down, towering over me. "You have destroyed my creation, my dream. That's why I'm leaving you and your little girlfriend here to rot in..."

Lee glances off to the side before his head jerks around. He searches frantically for Ria.

"You're the one who's gonna be left here rotting," Ria announces. She pops up from behind the desk.

Commander Lee spins around, only to be greeted by one of Ria's powerful Tele kicks to the face. The force from the edge of her boot connects under his chin and knocks him backward. His pistol flies out of his hand, clinking and sliding across the floor.

Lee scrambles for the loose weapon. He flips over, as he reaches out for it.

But Ria is quicker.

Her boot lunges out and lands on the top of the commander's bare hand. I hear an ominous, bone-crunching sound.

"Ahhh! Get off me, you witch!"

Commander Lee grabs hold of Ria's foot with his good hand and shoves her away. He flips her leg up, twisting it, yanking her off her feet. Ria lands on her side a few feet away. Lee takes full advantage of the situation. He pushes himself up and takes off running for the door.

I roll over with a grimace of pain. The handgun slides across the floor and lands in my hand as if I'm holding a magnet. Lying on my stomach, I grip the gun, lining the barrel end of the weapon up with the back of Lee's right leg. I pull the trigger.

Crack!

Lee stumbles. He shifts all of his weight to his other leg and limps off. A narrow trail of blood follows him.

I take aim again, firing, this time gripping the gun with both hands. I feel the recoil rocket down my arm as my entire limb vibrates painfully, shooting a bolt of lightning through my body.

Lee stumbles again, but this time forward, and lands on his stomach. His head turns to the side as I watch his last breath exit his lungs. His leg relaxes, before straightening out on its own.

It's over.

Commander Lee is dead.

CHAPTER 41

ROAR

I roll back over onto my back and let go of the smoking gun. The pistol clatters to the ground, echoing out loudly across the large office floor. Ria rushes up to me and grabs my hand.

"Nic! Nic! Are you okay?"

I blink my eyes, nodding in response. My ears still ring from the gunshots. "You saved me." I wince as I stare up at her big green eyes. Her tangled hair sticks to the side of her face. I reach up with my good arm and hook her fading pink bangs back behind her ear. I pull her inward lifting my head up. Our lips meet, teeth chatter. Suddenly, all the pain in my arm and shoulder is gone.

"Ten minutes to aerial attack."

The tranquil mechanical voice over the intercom pulls us apart.

Tick, tock, tick, tock, tick...

As the artificial clock sound resumes, Ria doesn't waste anymore time. She pulls me up into a seated position.

I close my eyes and choke back another groan.

Ria bends down on one knee and tears off the bottom half of her shirt, exposing her hourglass stomach. She folds the rag in half and wraps it around my open wound. "Our only hope is to get as low as possible and hope this place is designed to take a big hit." She keeps her eyes on her work before pulling the rag down across my arm, and I cry out loud this time.

A small kiss on the lips knocks out the pain and forces me to toughen up.

"Now if you're done being a big baby," she says with a smile, still hovering over me, "we have less than ten minutes to get down as many floors as possible." She smiles. "Or that's gonna be your last kiss."

I nod, take Ria's hand and follow her out of the office, down to the elevator. It hurts to run, so I sort of hobble after her. I grip onto my wounded arm as if it's about to break off from my torso at any moment.

Once inside, I sink to the floor, wedging my back up against the corner of the elevator. I lean to the side and rest my head up against the side of Ria's pant leg. Her hand drapes down, as she runs her fingers through my short hair in a soothing way. We rocket downward, dropping floor after floor, making it feel like we're moving much faster than before. My stomach begins to rise just as a loud bell dings over us. We jerk to a stop.

We're on the bottom level again. The arena.

It seems like every recruit, Tele soldier, and officer in the Compound is gathered in the arena. We step out and immediately bump into a large group of teenage boys all dressed in white. Everyone is silent, listening intently to someone address the crowd from the center.

"There's only one way out," a voice calls out in a deep island accent. "The tunnels."

Ria leads us through the massive crowd, weaving to the front where the group encircles Kingston and Rollins. August stands off to the side, hunched over, out of breath. Their clothes are torn; the three are covered in scratches and cuts from the battle.

August glances over and makes eye contact with Ria first. His eyes light up and he rushes over to us, taking her in his arms. "You're alive! I can't believe it!" He pulls her in for a kiss, but she pushes him away.

A hurt look washes over his face.

"Not now, August," she answers in a hushed voice, her eyes finding Kingston.

August glances over at the cloth wrapped around my arm, just now noticing me behind Ria. His eyes drop as he puts the pieces together in his head. He turns back to Ria and nods.

"They'll be expecting us to fly the drones out," Rollins adds, now addressing the few hundred Teles before him. He moves up a few paces to the center. "The tunnels are our only way out."

"I'm not following that traitor anywhere," someone calls out from behind me. All the heads turn and search for the voice, but it's quickly lost in the sea of blank faces.

"Yeah! I wouldn't even be here if it wasn't for him," another boy shouts out from across the room, this time a little closer to the front.

He wears the standard recruit's all-white uniform. He stares back at everyone with a prideful look on his face, arms folded.

"It's the risk we have to take." I jump in. I force myself to take a few more steps out into the middle of the circle, joining my brother and Kingston. Rollins flashes me a concerned look when he spots the blood-soaked cloth wrapped around my arm. I nod to him, reassuringly. "I was brought here unjustly, like each of you. We can sit here and argue about who we're gonna trust and who's a traitor, but that's only gonna get us one thing—dead." I glance around the room, letting it soak in. "If there's anyone here I shouldn't trust, it's the person who brought me here." I turn toward Kingston. "But what choice do I really have? What choice do you really have?"

"Five minutes to aerial strike."

"Commander Lee is dead," I continue, breaking through the eerie silence after the intercom's message ends. "I killed him!" I proudly raise my good arm halfway up in the air letting go of my wound. "For all those of you who followed him and his ways, there's nothing left for you here anymore." I scan the room, eyeing individual Tele soldiers still clutching their guns. "You're free. Follow us to freedom, back to your old life."

Someone in the middle of the floor roars, and it echoes loudly around the otherwise silent, massive room.

Within seconds, another recruit from the opposite side mimics it.

And then another and another.

The room fills with animalistic sounds, each person showing encouragement of and faith in Kingston.

I turn back toward the ex-recruiter again. "Lead the way."

CHAPTER 42

ALIVE

Just down the hall from the arena's entrance, we approach a door. It looks almost identical to the others in this place, but painted more of a dull red with no labels or markings on it. Just to the right, an elevator remains closed with a sign that reads: FOR OFFICIAL USE ONLY.

"They used to transport supplies through these tunnels back when this was a standard working Government base," Kingston informs us before placing his palm out, cleanly pulling the handle off the locked door. It drops to the ground.

He swings the dull painted door open and allows the darkness to suck in the bright light from our hallway. Just inside the entrance, only the small square platform is visible, followed by a dark dropping staircase that seems to go on forever. I stand slouched behind Kingston, my body beginning to tremble. I feel weak, tired. Sweat drips down my forehead; my body is feeling feverish all of a sudden. I stumble forward taking a step down, misjudging the distance. I reach out for the railing and catch myself from falling. Rollins grabs me by my shirt and pulls me back toward him.

"You okay?" he says, breathing into my ear, still grasping onto my shirt. "Just a little longer, Nic. We'll get you in a Healer as soon as we're outta here." His voice is disguised to sound confident, but I can sense his concern and disbelief.

*   *   *

The entire group makes it to the bottom before we move forward.

It's so dark now I can't see Kingston in front of me, even though I keep bumping him in the back. A few scattered groups of people talk behind us, but other than that everyone marches in silence. We have no clue how much time we have left before the air strike begins— minutes? Seconds? Without saying it, we all know the ceiling caving in over us will be our next and final announcement.

"Everyone listen up," Kingston calls out. He halts, then turns around and faces the group awaiting his next move. "We need to move as quickly as we can, but the tunnel narrows up ahead. Pair up. The last thing you want…"

Someone lets out a gasp only inches away, cutting off Kingston's speech. It takes me a couple of seconds to realize who it is.

"Oh no! Ren's not here," Ria screams, just remembering he didn't come down the stairwell with them. "Where's Ren?"

A few murmurs erupt behind us, most of them questioning the identity of Ren.

"He was in the control room before I went after Lee," I answer. "He's gotta be down here."

"Ren?" an unidentifiable voice calls out about ten people back.

"Ren?" Ria shouts. She cups her hands around her mouth.

No answer.

Somewhere off in the distance the sound of water drips, splashing down into a puddle. A random person close by coughs, followed by a distant, "Ouch, get off of my foot."

But no answer from Ren.

"I'm going back up," I announce to the group after no one else offers. "He's why we're free. We're not leaving him behind."

I sense Ria grabbing at my hand. She pulls me to her.

"You're in no shape to go," she says, squeezing.

Silence. No other volunteers.

"I'll get the boy," a deep, gruff voice announces only loud enough for the people surrounding him to hear.

August.

Ria releases her grip from my hand and turns toward the voice. "You get Ren and run right back," she says, her voice rising. "I can't lose you both."

August doesn't answer, but I feel the crowd sway to the side, allowing his large frame to push its way through the cluster of kids and climb back up the dark staircase. The door opens up at the top inviting the light back in only long enough for him to exit.

"You hurry back!" Ria calls out again, her voice lost in the walls surrounding us.

A few seconds pass, and everyone is thinking the same thing: if we wait for August to return, then we'll all be trapped down here in the attack. But if we leave, August and Ren might not be able to find their way out through the service tunnels.

"We have to keep moving," Kingston calls out to everyone after a few seconds of awkward silence. He makes an executive decision for the good of the group. "They'll catch up."

We enter the first tunnel, the narrowness of the rounded walls making us move in pairs. There's some sort of tracks running down the center of the ground that keeps tripping everyone up. It forces us to move much slower than we should. Following Kingston's lead, I walk side-by-side with Ria, her arm draped across my back edging me forward. A constant shallow stream of water washes over the tracks at our feet resulting in the sound of hundreds of boots splashing their way down the tunnel.

Boom!

A loud explosion goes off behind us making Ria jump and release her hold around me. I stumble to my knees, as I catch myself on the wall of the vibrating tunnel. A few muffled voices cry out in the distance, but everyone around us appears to be okay. I reach out with my good arm and feel the wall still trembling around us.

Boom!

Another explosion hits, again behind us, causing an even louder sound to erupt. Small pieces of the ceiling crumble down over our heads.

"August…Ren," Ria yelps.

"They're okay." I try to sound reassuring, but even I can hear the lie in my voice. I wipe some light debris out of my hair. "He had to have found—"

Boom! Boom! Boom! Boom!

The attack hits closer swallowing up my voice. The entire tunnel rumbles, shaking us like pennies in a can. I've never been in an earthquake before, but I can imagine this is sort of how it feels.

"Everyone okay?" Kingston calls out as soon as the rumbling stops. His voice shakes, not wanting to know the truth.

A few voices call out reassuringly, but we both know dead people can't answer.

"Just up ahead there should be supply carts. If they still work, they'll be able to take us the rest of the way." Kingston pauses. He waits to see if anyone objects. "We can fit up to eight bodies in each cart. Possibly more if we really squeeze in. Once the first group of carts reaches the outside, we'll…"

Boom! Boom! Boom!

Another set of explosions goes off overhead, rattling our tunnel again. The piercing sound of metal tearing over us stabs everyone in the ear and numerous people cry out in horror. Farther back in the tunnel, a large leak shoots down from the ceiling. The intense sound of rushing water over screams fills my ears.

"Everyone move!" an unidentifiable voice shouts out behind me. "The ceiling's coming down!"

There's a sudden mad rush of people behind us, pushing and shoving their way forward through the crowd to reserve a spot in one of the few carts. As the bombs continue to fall, more voices cry out, sounding like they're being trampled to death by the others behind them who are also trying to escape.

"Get in the first cart," Kingston yells out to me in a panicky voice. "There's no way we're gonna be able to get everyone out in one run."

Ria helps me hobble past a group of empty supply carts all lined up in a row on the tracks. Kingston helps Ria and Rollins into the cart, before climbing in himself. He pulls back on a long, thin lever in the front of the cart sending us forward down the tracks.

"It works," Kingston calls out.

He pulls even farther back on the lever, chugging us down the tracks like an old locomotive. As the cart picks up speed, the wind gently slaps me in the face forcing me to turn my head to the side. Distinct cries for help echo out behind us. I shudder and turn around. I grab Ria's hand in front of me and think of all the lost souls who will not make it out, but of two in particular.

I swallow hard, selfishly thankful I'm still alive and in this cart.

EPILOGUE

After breaking into a health clinic after hours and borrowing their Healer, the four of us find ourselves on the road in front of the house Rollins and I grew up in. The neighborhood is abnormally quiet, not a single person in sight. There are no cars moving on the road—not even a drone flying over.

"You think they're watching your place?" Ria asks. We all lean down behind an abandoned car in the neighborhood that hasn't moved in all of the years Rollins and I have lived here.

"I'd be more surprised if they weren't," Rollins responds. "These people do not take defeat well."

"And what about the NoMads?" Kingston adds. "Once they find out that some of us escaped, they're gonna be coming after us. It's clear they're not gonna stop at just destroying the Compound."

"Well, I'm going in," I say, straightening up. Thanks to the Healer, my body feels strong for the first time in a really long time. Before anyone can stop me, I dart across the street, leaping up the stairs two at a time.

I reach out for the handle, just now noticing the door has been left cracked open. Rollins grabs me by the back of my shoulder.

"Wait, Nic. Something isn't right."

Rollins moves around me and pushes the door open, taking the lead. He holds one hand out behind his back telling us to wait, but I follow anyway.

We enter to find the place ransacked. Tables and chairs are overturned. Loose papers litter the floor. Glass picture frames are broken and overturned. Even my father's work tablet with a now shattered screen lies flipped up in the center of the living room.

"What happened?" Ria questions. She gazes around the room.

"They were here, mate," Kingston says. He reads everyone else's thoughts. "They were looking for something...or someone."

"Who's they?" Ria asks again. Her voice rises up and cracks.

"The Government," Rollins answers monotone, his eyes searching the room. He turns around to face the group. His eyes shift back and forth, shoulders slumped. "Maybe the NoMads? There's no telling."

I break off from the others and make my way down the hall only to discover a faint trail of dried blood leading to my bedroom. The door is closed, but the trail continues into the room. I apprehensively push the door inward.

Without taking a step in, my eyes follow the trail of blood across the carpeted floor. It ends at the edge of the only window in the room. The top part of the glass is still intact; broken and jagged pieces hang down from the top like stalactites in caves leaving a big empty space where glass should be. I take a few small steps into the room just as a gust of wind blows in through the broken window giving me the chills.

"The place's empty," Rollins says, standing close behind me. The sudden sound of his voice causes me to flinch.

I turn to face the group, my eyes finding Rollins. "Whoever took them must have come when they were looking for us." I shake my head. "They're dead because of us. Because of me!"

"We don't know that," Rollins says. He steps forward and reaches out for my shoulder, but I defensively jerk it way.

"Maybe they got out?" Ria's tone is hopeful. "It looks like someone escaped through the window."

I turn away from the group and face the jagged pieces of glass. The image of my parents being tortured or even killed because of me keeps playing on a continuous loop in my head.

Down the hall, the front door creaks opens.

We all freeze.

Multiple pairs of heavy feet enter into the house, loudly stepping on already broken glass on the living room floor.

An image of a FootSoldier pops into my head. I turn to Rollins.

He lifts his finger up to his lips. "We have to leave, now," he says low and shrill, gritting his teeth. His eyes dart over to the only exit in the room—the broken window. One at a time, we climb out, jumping down behind the house.

"Now what?" I say, turning toward my brother.

"Now, we find the people who took our parents."

R. L. McDaniel

Born and raised in Florida, R. L. McDaniel currently resides in Tallahassee, Florida, where he has been teaching language arts to middle school students for over ten years. He enjoys playing the guitar and writing in his free time. *Levitation* is R. L. McDaniel's second published release. His first young adult novel, *The Big Hoot* was also recently published.

To learn more about R. L., please visit…

https://www.RLMcDaniel.com

https://www.facebook.com/RLMcDanielAuthor

Made in the USA
Charleston, SC
06 May 2016